Mia
in
the
mix

SIMON SPOTLIGHT

An imprint of Simon & Schuster Children's Publishing Division
1230 Avenue of the Americas, New York, New York 10020
Copyright © 2011 by Simon & Schuster, Inc.
First Simon Spotlight hardcover edition 2013
All rights reserved, including the right of reproduction
in whole or in part in any form.
SIMON SPOTLIGHT and colophon are registered trademarks
of Simon & Schuster, Inc.
Text by Tracey West
Chapter header illustrations and design by Laura Roode
For information about special discounts for bulk purchases, please contact
Simon & Schuster Special Sales
at 1-866-506-1949 or business@simonandschuster.com.
Manufactured in the United States of America 0413 FFG
First Edition
2 4 6 8 10 9 7 5 3 1
ISBN 978-1-4424-7491-8 (hc)
ISBN 978-1-4424-2277-3 (pbk)
ISBN 978-1-4424-2278-0 (eBook)
Library of Congress Catalog Card Number 2010940484

CUPCAKE DIARIES

Mia
in
the
mix

by coco simon

Simon Spotlight
New York   London   Toronto   Sydney   New Delhi

CHAPTER 1

An *Interesting* Remark

My name is Mia Vélaz-Cruz, and I hate Mondays.

I know, everybody says that, right? But I think I have some very compelling reasons for hating Mondays.

For example, every other weekend I go to Manhattan to see my dad. My parents are divorced, and my mom and I moved out to a town in the suburbs, an hour outside the city. I really like living with my mom, but I miss my dad a lot. I miss Manhattan, too, and all of my friends there. On the weekends I visit my dad, he drives me back to my mom's house late on Sunday nights. So it's weird when I wake up on Monday and I realize I'm not in New York anymore. Every two weeks I wake up all confused, which is not a good way to start a Monday.

Another reason I don't like Mondays is that it's the first day of the school week. That means five days of school until I get a day off. Five days of Mrs. Moore's hard math quizzes. And I have to wait all the way till the end of the week for Cupcake Friday. That's the day that either I or one of my friends brings in cupcakes to eat at lunch. That's how we formed the Cupcake Club. But I'll tell you more about that in a minute.

Lately I've been looking over a bunch of journal entries, and I've realized that when annoying things happen, they usually happen on a Monday. Back in May, my mom told me on a Monday night that we were moving out of New York. When I ruined my new suede boots because of a sudden rainstorm, it was on a Monday. And the last time I lost my cell phone, it was Monday. And when did I find it? Friday, of course. Because Friday is an awesome day.

Then there was that bad Monday I had a few weeks ago. It should have been a good Monday. A *great* Monday, even, because that was my first day back at school after the Cupcake Club won the contest.

Remember when I mentioned Cupcake Club? I'm in the club with my friends Katie, Alexis, and Emma. It started because we all eat lunch together, and on the first day of school Katie brought in this amazing peanut-butter-and-jelly cupcake that her mom made. Katie is a fabulous cupcake baker too, and she and her mom taught us all how to make them, so we decided to form our own club and make them together. Fun, right?

A little while after we formed the club, Principal LaCosta announced there was going to be a contest the day of the first school dance. There would be a big fund-raising fair in the school parking lot, and the group that raised the most funds would win a prize at the dance.

We hadn't really planned on participating in the fund-raiser, but then this other group in our class, the Popular Girls Club, kept telling everyone they were going to win. The leader of the group, Sydney, bragged that they had some "top-secret" idea that was going to blow everyone away. It's not like we're rivals or anything, but once we heard that, we decided to enter the contest too. Our idea was to sell cupcakes decorated with the school colors (that part was my idea).

The PGC's big secret ended up being a makeover booth, which would have been a cool idea except they weren't very good at doing makeovers. In fact, they were terrible at it. But we were very good at baking cupcakes. We sold two hundred cupcakes and won the contest. At the dance that night, Principal LaCosta gave us our prizes: four Park Street Middle School sweatshirts.

I know it's not a huge deal or anything, but it felt really good to win. Back at my old school, things were really competitive. Just about every kid took singing lessons or art lessons or violin lessons or French lessons. Everyone was good at something. It was hard to stand out there, and I never won a prize before. I was really happy that we won. It made me think maybe it wasn't bad that we moved out here.

Just before my mom picked me up the night of our big win, Alexis had an idea.

"We should all wear our sweatshirts to school on Monday," she said.

"Isn't that kind of like bragging?" Emma asked.

"We should do it," Katie said. "All the football guys wear their jerseys when they win a game. We won. We should be proud."

"Yes, definitely," I agreed. I mean, Katie was right. We should be proud. Making two hundred cupcakes is a lot of work!

Except for one problem. I don't do sweatshirts. I'm sorry, but the last time I wore one I was five, and it made me look like a steamed dumpling. They

4

are all lumpy and the sleeves are always too long.

Even though I wanted to show how proud I was of winning, I also knew there was no way I could wear that sweatshirt on Monday. I really care about what I wear, probably because my mom used to work for a big fashion magazine. So fashion is in my blood. But I also think clothes are a fun way to express yourself. You can seriously tell a lot about a person by what they choose to wear, like their mood for instance. And so to *me* a sweatshirt just says "I'm in the mood to sweat!"

I told Mom about my sweatshirt issue on the drive home.

"Mia, I'm surprised by you," she said. "You're great at transforming your old clothes into new and amazing creations. Think of your old school uniform. You made that look great and like you every day. If you *had* to wear a sweatshirt, I'd bet you could come up with something really cool and great."

Mom was right, to be honest, and I was a little surprised I hadn't thought of it first. Our old school uniform was terrible: ugly plaid skirts with plain white, itchy tops. But you could wear a sweater or a jacket and any shoes, so you could get pretty creative with it and not look gross on a daily basis. That's

5

one of the good things about my new school—you can wear whatever you want. Inspired, I sat at my sewing table the next day and cut up the sweatshirt. I turned it into a cool hobo bag, the kind with a big pouch and a long strap. I added a few cool studs to the strap and around the school logo to funk it up a little. I was really proud of how it looked.

On Monday morning I picked out an outfit to go with the bag: a denim skirt, a blue knit shirt with a brown leather belt around the waist, and a dark-gray-and-white-striped-blazer. I rolled up the sleeves of the blazer, then put the bag over my shoulder and checked out my reflection in the long mirror attached to my closet.

Too much blue, I decided. I changed the blue shirt to a white one, then changed the belt to a braided silver belt and checked again.

Better, I thought. I pulled my long black hair back into a ponytail. *Maybe a headband . . . or maybe braid it to the side . . .*

"Mia! You'll be late for your bus!" Mom called from downstairs.

I sighed. I'm almost always late for the bus, no matter how early I wake up. I decided to leave my hair down and hurried downstairs.

Taking a bus to school is something I still need

to get used to. When I went to my school in New York, I took the subway. A lot of people don't like the subway because of how crowded it is, but I love it. I like to study the people and see what they're wearing. Everyone has their own distinct style and things that they're into. And there are all kinds of people on a subway—old people, moms with little kids, kids going to school like me, people from the suburbs going to work. Also, on the subway, nobody whispers about you behind your back like they do on the bus. Nobody makes loud burping noises either, like Wes Kinney does every single day in the back of the school bus, which is extremely disgusting.

The best thing about the bus, though, is that my friend Katie takes it with me. That's how we met, on the first day of school. Her best friend was sup-posed to ride with her, but she walked to school instead, so I asked Katie to sit with me. I felt bad for Katie, but it was lucky for me. Katie is really cool.

When Katie got on the bus that morning she was wearing her Park Street sweatshirt with lightly ripped jeans and her favorite blue canvas sneakers. Her wavy brown hair was down. She has natural highlights, as if she hung out every day at the beach.

If I didn't know Katie, I would have guessed she was from California.

"Hey!" Katie said, sliding into the seat next to me. She pointed to her sweatshirt. "I still can't believe we won!"

"Me either," I said. "But we did make some really fabulous cupcakes."

"Totally," Katie agreed. Then she frowned. "Did you forget to wear your shirt?"

"I'm wearing it," I told her. I showed her the bag. "What do you think?"

"No way!" Katie grabbed it to get a closer look. "Did your mom do this?"

"I did," I replied.

"That is awesome," Katie said. "I didn't know you could sew. That's got to be harder than making cupcakes."

I shrugged. "I don't know. It just takes practice."

Braaap! Wes Kinney made a big fake burp just then. His friends all started laughing.

"That is so gross," Katie said, shaking her head.

"Seriously!" I agreed.

This Monday was starting out okay (except for the part when I didn't get to wear my headband). But it got annoying pretty fast in homeroom.

None of my Cupcake Club friends are in my

homeroom, but I do know some kids. There's George Martinez, who's kind of cute and really funny. He's in my science and social studies classes too. There's Sophie, who I like a lot. But she sits next to her best friend, Lucy, and in homeroom they're always in a huddle, whispering to each other.

Then there is Sydney Whitman and Callie Wilson. Sydney is the one who started the Popular Girls Club. Callie is in the club too, and she's also the girl who used to be Katie's best friend. I can see why, because she's nice, like Katie.

Katie, Alexis, and Emma all think Sydney is horrible. They say she's always making mean comments to them. She's never said anything really mean to me. And to be honest, I like the way she dresses. She has a really good sense of fashion, which is something we have in common. Like today, she was wearing a scoop-neck T-shirt with a floral chiffon skirt, black leggings, and an awesome wraparound belt that had a large pewter flower as the buckle. So sometimes I think, you know, that maybe we could be friends. Don't get me wrong—the girls in the Cupcake Club are my BFFs, and I love them. But none of them are into fashion the way I am.

Sydney and Callie sit right across from me. Callie gave me a smile when I sat down.

"Those were great cupcakes you guys made on Saturday," Callie told me.

"Thanks," I said.

I thought I saw Sydney give Callie a glare. But when she turned to me, she was smiling too.

"That was a really *interesting* dress you wore to the dance, Mia," Sydney said.

Hmm. I wasn't sure what "interesting" meant. I had worn a minidress with black, purple, and turquoise panels, a black sequined jacket, and black patent leather peep toe flats. "Perfectly chic," my mom had said.

"Thanks."

"Very . . . red carpet maybe?" Sydney went on. "Although, I was reading this really *interesting* article in *Fashionista* magazine all about choosing the right outfit for the right event. You know, like how being *overdressed* can be just as bad as being underdressed."

I knew exactly what Sydney was doing. She was insulting me, but in a "nice" way. Sort of. I know my outfit might have been a little too sophisticated for a middle school dance, but so what? I liked it.

"There's no such thing as being overdressed," I replied calmly. "That's what my mom taught me. She used to be an editor at *Flair* magazine." Then

I opened up my notebook and began to sketch. I don't normally brag about my mother's job like that, but I didn't know what to say to Sydney.

"Wow!" said Callie. "*Flair*? That's so cool! Isn't that cool?" She turned to Sydney, who looked uninterested. "We read that all the time at Sydney's house. Her mom gets it."

Sydney opened her math book and pretended to start reading.

"You looked really great!" said Callie, like she was trying to make up for Sydney. I honestly didn't really care if they liked it or not. I thought I looked good and that outfit made me feel great.

I wasn't mad at Sydney—just annoyed. Which is not a fabulous way to start the day.

But what can you expect from a Monday?

CHAPTER 2

Meat Loaf Monday Continues

So, the next Monday-esque thing happened at lunchtime. I sit at a table with Katie, Alexis, and Emma. Katie always brings her lunch, like me, and Alexis and Emma always get lunch from the cafeteria.

When I got to the table, Katie was already eating her sandwich. I opened up my new bag and realized I'd forgotten to put my lunch bag inside this morning.

"This is seriously disappointing," I said with a sigh. Luckily, I always carry a few dollars around in case of an emergency. I looked at Katie. "Forgot my lunch. I'll be back in a minute."

Katie's mouth was full of peanut butter, so she nodded in reply. I walked over to the line and found myself right behind Alexis and Emma. They're best friends, but they're both really different. Alexis has reddish wavy hair and likes to talk a lot. Emma was taller, with straight blond hair and big blue eyes. She's a little bit shy, and definitely quieter than Alexis. They're both supernice though.

Today they were both wearing their Park Street sweatshirts. Alexis wore hers with a white denim skirt and a white headband in her hair, and Emma had on cute blue denim leggings.

"I forgot my lunch," I told them. "What are they having today?"

"Monday is meat loaf day," Alexis told me. "With mashed potatoes and string beans."

"Oh," I said. I am not a big fan of meat loaf. Of course, Monday would have to be meat loaf day.

"It's not bad," Emma said, noticing my face. "You can get a salad instead if you want."

That cheered me up. "I'll do the salad, definitely!"

"So, did you forget to wear your sweatshirt?" Alexis asked me.

"No." I held out my bag. "I transformed it, but I'm still wearing it, see?"

I wasn't expecting Alexis's reaction. "You cut it up?" She sounded a little upset.

"Well, I had to, to make the bag," I explained.

Alexis frowned. "It's just, I thought we were going to wear them together, like a team," she said.

"Oh!" I said, because I didn't really know what to say. Was she mad at me?

"But it's a nice bag," Emma said, giving Alexis a look.

"Thanks," I said. "And we are a team. It's just, I don't like sweatshirts. It's hard to look good in a sweatshirt, you know? They're so puffy and lumpy."

I felt bad as soon as I said the words. "I mean, you guys look great, I just don't like how I look in them," I said quickly.

Alexis turned away. "Time to order."

I felt really terrible as I took my salad from the cold shelf. The three of us were quiet as we walked back to the table.

"I've been so alone!" Katie said in a funny, dramatic way. "Thank goodness you're here at last! Hey, did you check out Mia's bag? Isn't it cool? Maybe you could make one for me, too. This sweatshirt is *hot*!"

And just like that, everything was all right. Katie is like that. She's so sweet and funny, it's hard to be in a bad mood when you're around her.

But I still felt bad about what I said. And there was a part of me that wished Alexis, you know, got me better. Like my best friend, Ava, who lives in Manhattan. All I'd have to do is say the word "sweatshirt," and she'd know what I was talking about: steamed dumpling.

I think that's the biggest problem I have here at Park Street Middle School. I don't feel like anyone really gets me. Not like Ava does, anyway. The Cupcake Club is great, but Ava has known me since first grade. She knows everything about me. I try not to think about it too much, but it can be a bit lonely sometimes.

The Monday madness continued after school. When I got home, my dogs, Tiki and Milkshake, ran up to greet me like they always do. They're little, fluffy, white dogs with black noses, and I think they are perfectly adorable. Mom and I adopted them after the divorce when we went to live in a new apartment, one that allowed dogs. After I petted them both, I went over to my mom's office to talk to her.

Mom's starting up her own fashion consulting business, so she works out of the house, which is nice. I see her a lot more now.

But Mom wasn't there. Then I heard Eddie's voice behind me.

"Sorry, Mia. Your mom had to go into the city

for a meeting. She won't be home till late," he said.

Eddie is my soon-to-be stepdad. Mom and I live in the house with him and my soon-to-be stepbrother, Dan. Eddie is a lawyer whose law firm is over in the next town. When my mom left her job to start up her consulting company, Eddie asked her to marry him. They're getting married this spring.

"How late?" I asked.

"I'm not sure," he said. "But there's good news! I'll be cooking tonight. You're in for a real treat. It's my famous mystery meat loaf!"

It looked like I was not going to escape meat loaf, no matter how hard I tried. "Why is it a *mystery* meat loaf?" I asked.

"Because the recipe is very mysterious," Eddie said in a fake mysterious voice. Then he made spooky noises. *"Oooh, whooo . . ."*

Eddie is always trying to make me laugh. Sometimes I do, but it's not easy. His jokes can be pretty awful at times.

"Just let me know when it's time to set the table," I told him.

I walked up the stairs to my room, and Milkshake and Tiki followed me. Before Mom and I moved in with Eddie and Dan, the room was supposed to be a guest room, but it was mostly filled with boxes of stuff that Dan had when he was a kid. It has weird flowery wallpaper, like something you'd find in an old lady's house. Eddie keeps saying he'll paint it, but he's always busy. So is Mom. Between getting ready for the wedding and starting her new business, she doesn't have a lot of extra time.

So for now, I'm stuck with the room with the weird wallpaper. My room at my dad's apartment is much more me. We decorated it with a Parisian Chic theme. The walls are pale pink with black-and-white accents. My headboard is this twisted flowery iron, and my bedspread and pillows have a cool black-and-white pattern on them. I have a really pretty white vanity where I can keep all my hair stuff, and I can actually sit down to do my hair in the morning. One day I can put makeup in there . . . if my mom ever lets me wear anything other than lip gloss.

In *this* room the bed has a green quilt and the curtains are blue and they don't match at all. My old quilt doesn't fit because this bed is big—a double bed—which is nice, but the quilt is ugly. There's no vanity, but there's an old wooden dresser, which is *brown*, and a desk for my computer and a small table for my sewing machine in the

17

corner. My table with my sewing machine on it is the only piece of furniture from my mom's old apartment. Since everything is so much bigger at Eddie's house, Mom said it was a perfect chance for us to leave my old furniture behind and update and redo my bedroom. Which she promises to do soon. But until that happens, I've just been covering up the wallpaper with fashion spreads that I tear out of my favorite magazines. It's not great, but at least it covers up most of those ugly flowers.

The one good thing about this room, though, is the closet—it's three times the size of my closet in New York. Which is good, because I keep most of my clothes at this house anyway.

The way my room is decorated isn't the only thing I don't like about it. The other bad thing is that it's next to Dan's room. And Dan loves heavy metal music—the loud kind, where the lead singer screams like there's a fire or something. He listens to it all the time.

Like right now. The loud music (if you can call it music) blared from behind Dan's door, shaking the walls and the floor. All I wanted to do was call Ava, but I'd never be able to hear her on the line.

I knocked on Dan's door. "Dan, can you turn it down, please?"

It was no use. He couldn't hear me. So I went into my room, sat on my bed, and stuck in my earbuds. I pressed play on my iPod, and a song by my favorite singer filled my ears—but I swear I could still see the walls shaking.

Tiki and Milkshake curled up in the purple dog bed I keep for them in my room. Then I texted Ava.

FabMia: Miss you! How's ur Monday going?
Avaroni: Not good. U know those boots I got last week? The heel fell off rite in the middle of school! I almost fell.
FabMia: Oh no! U okay?
Avaroni: :(I hate Mondays!
FabMia: Me 2!
Avaroni: Hey, gotta go. Me n Delia r going to that xhibit at the Met.
FabMia: Jealous!
Avaroni: Peace out.
FabMia: Talk soon. Bye.

I clicked off the phone with a frown. I was happy for Ava, but I was jealous too. If I were still living in Manhattan, I would be going to that exhibit. I didn't even know who Delia was, either. I think Ava told me she met her in French class or something.

So . . . no Mom. No Ava. And mystery meat loaf

in my near future. I couldn't wait until Monday was over.

I took off my shoes and searched for my sketch-book, which I found under a pillow at the foot of my bed. I opened it up and started to sketch an idea for a dress I'd been thinking about. As I moved the pencil across the page, I didn't notice the shaking walls or the mysterious smell of meat loaf wafting up the stairs.

That's how it always feels when I sketch. The whole world melts away. And that is a nice feeling, especially on a Monday.

CHAPTER 3

We're in Business!

For the record, let me just say that "mystery meat loaf" probably got its name because it's a mystery why anyone would eat it. But I didn't want to hurt Eddie's feelings, so I didn't tell him that. Instead I managed to sneak most of it to Tiki and Milkshake, who always hang out under the table while we're eating, hoping to get some scraps.

Thankfully that was the last annoying thing that happened on Monday. And the next day, Tuesday, was much better, of course.

To start with, even though Mom got home late, she still packed me a lunch, and I didn't forget it this time. My mom made my favorite: a turkey and Brie wrap with a side of red grapes. Yum!

While we were eating, Alexis started talking

about the school fund-raiser. People were still talking about it.

"You won't believe what just happened in French class," she said, sticking a fork into her spaghetti. "Before class, Mademoiselle Girard came up to me and congratulated me on the Cupcake Club winning the contest. Sydney was standing right there, and she gave me *such* a nasty look!"

"I kind of feel bad for them," said Katie. "I know they worked really hard on that makeover booth."

"It's a shame that their makeovers were so terrible," I added. "Remember when Sophie showed us what Bella had done to her? She had on so much white makeup that she looked like a clown."

Alexis shrugged. "Well, I think their problem was that they didn't work out the numbers first. Each makeover must have cost five dollars if you add up all the makeup they bought, but took twenty minutes to finish. That's only fifteen dollars an hour. But our cupcakes cost two dollars each, and we could sell one every minute. Do the math."

"Do I have to?" Katie groaned.

I've never known anybody who loves numbers as much as Alexis. It's probably because her parents are accountants. Actually, that's something we have in common, in a way. My mom works in fashion, and

22

I love fashion. I wondered if I would be like Alexis if my mom had been an accountant. . . .

"I hope the girls in the PGC don't feel too bad," Katie said, and I knew she was thinking about Callie. "At least they tried."

While we were talking, Ms. Biddle came up to our table. She teaches science, and we all agree that she's the best teacher in our grade. She's really funny, and she has cool blond hair that she spikes up with gel. Every day she wears a different science T-shirt. See? Her clothes tell me she likes science! Today she was wearing a shirt with the periodic table of the elements on it.

"Hey there," she said. "Do you young entrepreneurs mind if I talk to you for a minute?"

I know what "entrepreneur" means because my mom is one. It's somebody who starts their own business.

"Sure," Katie said.

Ms. Biddle slid into the empty chair at the end of the table. "Next Saturday—not this one, but the next one—I have to throw a baby shower for my sister. She loves cupcakes. And I have never made a cupcake in my life that wasn't burnt or dry as toast. So I was wondering if the Cupcake Club would like the job."

"We would love it!" Katie said quickly. "I mean, if everyone agrees."

"Isn't baking cupcakes just like chemistry?" Alexis asked. "I thought you'd be good at making cupcakes."

"You're right," Ms. Biddle admitted. "Baking is a lot like science. It's a total embarrassment. I can make anything in a science lab, but put me in a kitchen and I lose all of my mojo."

"We should definitely do it," I said.

"I think so too," Emma chimed in.

Alexis took a small notebook out of her backpack. "Can you please give us the details? Time? Place? Number of cupcakes?"

Ms. Biddle gave Alexis the address. "I think four dozen should do it. How much do you charge?"

"Two dollars per cupcake is our normal price," Alexis answered. "But you qualify for the teacher discount. That's half price at one dollar each."

"Perfect!" Ms. Biddle said with a grin. She stood up to leave.

"One more thing," I said. Alexis is good with numbers, but she'd forgotten the most important detail. "What kind of cupcake do you want? And do you want any special colors?"

"We don't know yet if the baby is a boy or girl, so

the decorations are going to be yellow and green. I guess the cupcakes should match," said Ms. Biddle. "But you can make any flavor you want, as long as it's delicious."

"They will be!" Katie promised. "Thanks so much."

After Ms. Biddle walked away, Katie let out a happy squeal.

"This is amazing!" Katie said. "Our first paying job!"

"Don't forget we're doing the PTA luncheon in the spring too," Emma added.

"This will be good practice," I pointed out.

"I hope you don't mind me offering the teacher discount," Alexis said. "I thought it might help us drum up more business."

"No, that was a good idea," Katie told her.

"And it's a nice thing to do for teachers," Emma added.

Alexis tapped her pencil on her notebook page. "We should still be able to make a nice profit. I'm still working out how much it costs per cupcake. Our parents donated the ingredients for the fundraiser, but we'll have to start paying for our own now."

"How will we buy the ingredients if we don't

have any money to start with?" Emma wondered.

"Maybe my mom could lend it to us," Katie suggested. She always has good ideas for how to solve problems. "Then we could pay her back when Ms. Biddle pays us."

"That could work," Alexis agreed.

I had been thinking about what Alexis said about profit. I was excited because making cupcakes is fun, but the idea of making some extra money was pretty nice. I could finally buy that great pair of jeans that Mom said were too expensive.

"So what will we do with our profits?" I asked, thinking about how those jeans would look really good with my favorite shirt.

"We should probably save some to make more cupcakes, and then divide up the rest," Alexis replied. "But we should talk about it."

"Can we have a meeting tomorrow?" Katie asked.

"Good idea," I said. "Maybe we could meet at the food court at the mall. Then we could go window-shopping afterward."

I'll find any excuse to go to the mall. It makes living in the suburbs a lot more bearable.

But Alexis wrinkled her nose. "The food court is too noisy for a meeting, don't you think?"

"Why don't we meet at my house? We haven't met at my house in a long time," Emma said.

Alexis rolled her eyes. "Your little brother is *way* noisier than the mall."

"No, let's go to Emma's!" Katie said.

I was disappointed we weren't going to the mall, but I was out-voted.

"Cool," I said.

Katie turned to me. "Joanne's picking me up tomorrow. I'll ask my mom if she can take us to Emma's house."

"Sounds good," I said. I was feeling pretty excited about the whole thing.

The Cupcake Club makes living out here a whole lot easier.

CHAPTER 4

Emma's House

After school the next day I met Katie on the school steps. Park Street Middle School is a big concrete building with two sports fields in the back, a little kids' park on one side, and trees on the other side. There's a big, round driveway in front where the school buses line up. If someone is picking you up in a car, you have to follow the sidewalk down to the street.

"I think I see Joanne," Katie said, pointing to a shiny red car.

Katie's mom is a dentist, and Joanne works in the office there. Most days, Joanne picks up Katie from school and brings her back to the dentist's office until Mrs. Brown gets off work. Katie's mom is really nice, but she's really overprotective, too.

"I'm so glad we have a meeting today," Katie told

me as we walked. "Otherwise I'd be stuck in a dentist's office."

"That does sound really boring," I admitted.

"It is," Katie said. "But you know what I hate the most? That dentist's office smell. I don't think I'll ever get used to it."

"I know what you mean," I told her. "Every time I smell it, it reminds me of that time I got my cavity filled. That was seriously painful!"

"You should go to my mom," Katie said. "Her patients all say it hardly hurts at all when she works on them. Although you should hear her lecture about the importance of flossing. Now *that's* painful."

Joanne stuck her head out of the car window when she saw us approach. "Hey, girlfriends! How are you doing today?"

"Good," Katie and I answered at the same time.

We got into the backseat together. Joanne's red car is really sporty, and she always plays good music. It's much better than taking the bus.

"So what's going on at Emma's today?" Joanne asked.

"A Cupcake Club meeting," Katie replied. "We got hired by Ms. Biddle to bake cupcakes."

"Is that the cool science teacher you told me about?" Joanne asked.

Katie nodded. "Yeah, she's really nice."

Joanne sighed. "I wish I was going to a cupcake meeting. Instead, I've got to go back to the office and try to explain to Mr. Michaels why he can't put his false teeth in the dishwasher."

Katie and I giggled. Then Joanne pulled up in front of Emma's house. "Have fun," she said. "Katie, your mom will get you on her way home."

Katie and I thanked Joanne and walked up to Emma's front door. She lives in a two-story white house with a porch that wraps all the way around it. It's a really pretty house, except for the big pile of sports equipment in the driveway. There were bats and gloves and basketballs, even a lacrosse stick. There's also a basketball hoop in the driveway, and Emma's two older brothers, Matt and Sam, were shooting baskets with their friends.

The ball bounced on the walkway in front of us, and Sam, who's a senior, ran up to get it.

He stopped when he saw me. "Hey, aren't you Dan's little sister?"

"I'm going to be his *step*sister," I replied. Katie kind of gave me a look. But I wasn't really Dan's sister. Or Dan's *real* sister. I don't know, it's all confusing. It was a lot simpler when I was an only child.

"Yo, Sam! Over here!" one of the boys called.

Sam ran off without another word. Then Emma opened the front door.

"Come on in. Alexis has us set up in the kitchen," she said with a smile.

We walked through the living room, stepping over a giant city of blocks surrounded by plastic dinosaurs. Emma's little brother, Jake, was standing in front of the TV, watching a cartoon. I think he's completely adorable.

Emma turned off the TV. "Jake, come into the kitchen with us."

Jake frowned. "I wanna watch TV!"

Jake is completely adorable—when he's not crying and whining. Emma says that happens a lot, but he'll grow out of it.

Emma gave us an apologetic look. "Mom's at work," she explained. "She'll be back soon. I said I didn't mind watching him since we're not baking today. He'll be good."

"I wanna watch TV!" Jake demanded.

Emma took his hand. "Later, Jake. We're going to color now."

That seemed to satisfy him. Emma led us all into the kitchen, where Alexis had a bunch of papers spread out on the table.

"Hey," she said. "So I've worked out how much

it will cost us to make each cupcake if we use basic ingredients. We need to figure out what we're making in case we need to add other stuff."

That's Alexis for you. She loves to get right down to business. We all sat down at the table, and Emma sat next to Jake. She gave him a banana and opened up his dinosaur coloring book.

"I was thinking about that," Katie said. "Ms. Biddle said the decorations will be yellow and green. So maybe the cupcake flavor could sort of match. You know, like a banana or a lemon cupcake."

I glanced over at Jake. Gooey banana was smeared on his face. At that moment the thought of eating a banana cupcake didn't sound too appetizing.

"How about lemon?" I asked. "Lemon is nice."

Alexis started writing in her notebook. "I'll have to check on the price of lemons and add that to our cost. How many will we need, Katie?"

Katie shrugged. "I'll have to look at the recipe."

"And what about the icing?" Alexis asked. "Should we make the icing green and yellow too?"

"I don't know about the green," Katie said thoughtfully. "It's a fun color for Easter, or to make monster cupcakes. But it might not be good for a baby shower."

"Yellow is pretty," Emma said.

Jake tugged on her shirt. "Color with me!"

"Sorry he's so loud," Emma said apologetically, and she picked up a crayon to color with her brother.

"Hey, he's way quieter than Dan, and Dan is sixteen," I said.

"Thanks," Emma said with a smile. "I sometimes feel like an alien or something around all these boys. Like I never fit in . . ."

"Tell me about it," I said. "Living with boys is hard!"

Katie shrugged; she was an only child. And Alexis had an older sister who had really nice clothes, so that had to be good for her.

"It's not easy," said Emma. She smiled at me. Maybe Emma could help me learn to deal with Dan.

"So, I googled baby shower themes last night," I said, pulling out pictures from my backpack. "I printed out some pictures."

I put my favorite picture on the table. It showed a green and yellow baby shower. Everything was set up on a white table sprinkled with real yellow flowers. There were no cupcakes, but in the center was a white layer cake decorated with yellow flowers and green leaves.

"Ooh, that's so pretty!" Emma said, and Alexis and Katie nodded in agreement.

"So maybe we could use white icing, and decorate it with flowers and leaves on top," I suggested.

Katie looked closely at the picture. "Cream cheese icing would be nice with the lemon. But how would we make the flowers?"

"I did some research," I said. Decorating the cupcakes is my favorite part. "There are so many amazing websites that sell cupcake decorations. I saw some pretty flower molds. You melt chocolate in any color you want, and then you get a little candy flower. Or we could get flowers made out of sparkly sugar. Those could be pretty."

Jake put down his crayon. "I want a cupcake!" he cried. Emma ignored him and kept coloring.

"Mia, you can be in charge of the flowers," Alexis said. "And Katie, can you shop for the ingredients? Your mom's going to lend us the money, right?"

Katie nodded. "She said it's no problem. She said it's okay to bake at our house, too, if we want. We should probably do it next Friday night so the cupcakes are fresh on Saturday."

"We could bake at my house this time if you want," I suggested. "We have one of those double ovens in our kitchen. We might be able to fit all four cupcake pans in at once. Then it won't take so long."

"Awesome!" Katie said.

"Mia, will you be home next Friday, or will you be at your dad's?" Alexis asked.

"I'm going to my dad's this weekend," I replied, "so I'll be here." I thought about it for a second; yep, that was right. Sometimes even I can't keep track of my own schedule.

Katie got a weird look on her face. She always does whenever I mention I'm seeing my dad. I know her parents are divorced, because Alexis told me once. But Katie never gets to see her dad like I do, though I'm not sure why. When I heard that, I tried to imagine what it would feel like if I didn't get to see my dad every other weekend. It'd really hurt.

"It looks like we have a plan, then," Alexis said, scribbling some more in her notebook.

Then a squishy piece of banana flew through the air. It landed right on the notebook page!

"Jake!" Emma scolded.

"Sorry, Lexi," Jake apologized. "It's slippery!"

Everyone laughed—even Alexis. I told you that kid was cute!

CHAPTER 5

A Surprise at the Mall

We hung out at Emma's house for a little while, playing dinosaurs with Jake. Then I got a text from my mom.

Be there in 5. Ready for a girls' night out?

I texted back.

Always ready.

Whenever we can, my mom and I go out to dinner—just the *two* of us. Eddie and Dan do not get to come. Tonight Mom suggested we go to the mall and then eat at the Italian restaurant there. Of course, I was happy to agree.

Mom texted me when she pulled up out front,

and I said good-bye to Emma, Katie, and Alexis. Then I ran outside and climbed into the front seat.

"It smells good in here," I said.

"New perfume," Mom told me. "One of my clients gave it to me. It's called Blue Mystery. What do you think?"

"It smells better than Eddie's mystery meat loaf," I replied.

"Oh, no. Did he make that for you Monday night?"

I nodded.

"Then you definitely deserve dinner out tonight," Mom said. "You poor thing!"

I can't figure Mom out sometimes. She agrees with me that Eddie's cooking is sometimes terrible, and so are his jokes. But she still wants to marry him. *What's up with that?* I mean, she could have stayed with my dad, who tells good jokes and makes really good chicken in tomato sauce.

When we got to the Westgrove Mall, Mom looked at her watch. "We have an hour until dinner," she said. "I was thinking we could stop in the candle shop first."

"Seriously?" I asked. "Mom, you have every flavor of candle that place makes."

"You mean scent, not flavor," Mom corrected

me. "And you're wrong. They just released their Midnight Jasmine collection."

I sighed. "Do we have to? All those *scents* make me dizzy."

"Isn't that clothing store you like a few doors down?" Mom asked. "Why don't you go there, and I'll catch up with you."

"Yes!" I cheered.

We rode the escalator up to the second floor. Katie says the mall is like a big maze, but it didn't take me long to figure out how to get around. My favorite clothing store, Icon, is three doors down from the candle shop, right between the Japanese pottery shop and the place that sells skater clothes.

My mom dropped me off by the entrance, and I walked inside. Before I got a chance to look around, I heard a familiar voice.

"Oh my gosh, oh my gosh, oh my gosh, this sweater is soooooooo cute!"

It was Maggie Rodriguez, one of the girls in the Popular Girls Club. I don't know Maggie that well, but it's easy to see that she has *a lot* of energy. She's always rushing around the hallways, late for class, and her frizzy brown hair is always flying around her face.

Maggie was holding up a really cute sweater. It was red, but not a bright red, more like a muted red, which was really nice. There were white designs on it, so it looked kind of like a ski sweater, but it wasn't big and bulky, like a sweatshirt. Plus it had a cool zipper down the front.

She was showing the sweater to Bella, another girl in the PGC. Bella is into the whole vampire thing. I think she uses a straightener on her auburn hair, and she wears pale makeup and a lot of dark colors. Katie told me her name used to be Brenda, but she changed it to Bella like the girl in that vampire movie. I think she made a good choice—Bella is a great name.

I walked up to them. "Hey, that's a really cute sweater," I said.

Maggie whirled around. "Isn't it? I can't believe they have the winter clothes out now. I haven't even started planning my winter wardrobe yet. This is terrible! I have to start, like, right now!"

Callie stepped out from behind a clothing rack. "Calm down, Maggie. There's plenty of time," she said with a smile.

Now I could see that Sydney was nearby, looking through the jeans stacked against the wall. It's hard to miss Sydney—she's tall, has blond hair that's perfectly straight and glossy, and teeth so sparkling white, she could star in a toothpaste commercial.

She must have seen me, too, but she didn't say anything just then.

"Where'd you find the sweater?" I asked Maggie. "That would look so good with these jeans I'm dying to get."

"Over here," Maggie said, rushing off. I followed her, and Bella and Callie came with us.

"Does it come in black?" Bella asked.

"I think so," Maggie said.

I pulled one of the sweaters off of the rack and held it up to me. "So cute," I said. "Last week I saw a spread in *Teen Style* that had tons of sweaters like this. It's the must-have for winter. They showed how you can wear it all these different ways, like even with flowy skirts. It was really amazing."

"I saw that too." It was Sydney. "With big furry boots, right?"

I nodded. "Yeah, that's the one!"

"It looked really great!" said Sydney. "Only the furry boots looked a little like a big gorilla or something."

I laughed. "They totally did!"

Maggie whipped out her smart phone and started frantically searching for the article online. "Seriously! Nobody tells me anything!"

"I saw some layered skirts back there," Callie said.

"Thanks," I told her. "I have got to check this out."

I grabbed the sweater and headed to the back of the room to find a skirt that would match.

Maggie started freaking out. "Oh wow, that is so supercute! You have to try it on!"

I didn't argue. I went into a dressing room and started trying on the outfit. As I was zipping up the sweater, it hit me.

I was having fun—with the Popular Girls Club!

Back in Manhattan, Ava and I would go into stores and try on clothes all the time. We didn't always buy something, but it was just fun to try on different styles. Sometimes we went into really fancy stores for inspiration. We would look at the displays and see what different designers were doing for each season. Then we'd go home and try to figure out how we could create the same look with the stuff we already had. Some of the stuff we came up with was pretty crazy and looked ridiculous, but sometimes we came up with something really cool.

I stepped out of the dressing room with the outfit on.

"What do you think?" I asked.

"I really like it," Callie said.

"It looks just like the magazine," Sydney said. "Without the gorilla part."

Bella nodded. "Just like the magazine," she echoed.

That's when my mom walked in, carrying a bag from the candle shop.

"Nice outfit," she said.

"Mom, this is Callie, Sydney, Maggie, and Bella," I said.

"Nice to meet you," Mom said.

Maggie ran over to Mom's bag and started sniffing the air. "Is that the new Midnight Jasmine collection? I have been dying to smell that."

"I'd better go change," I said. "Mom, isn't this the *perfect* outfit for winter?"

Okay, so I was hinting big-time. Mom doesn't always give in. But it was worth a try.

"Hmm, I saw something like that recently in a Damien Francis show," Mom said. "I wonder if I could get some samples from him. He owes me one. Who knows, maybe he has your size?" she said with a wink.

In the fashion industry, designers make samples of their clothes that they can show to shoppers for the big stores that want to buy them. Sometimes they sell them really cheap at things called sample sales, and sometimes they give them to friends—like my mom. Okay, so it wasn't a total yes or definite about the outfit, but I'll take it!

"No way. You know Damien Francis?" Maggie asked.

"He's an old friend of mine. I've worked with him a lot," Mom replied.

"That is sooo completely awesome!" Maggie gushed.

"When you worked at *Flair*?" Callie asked. I was kind of surprised she remembered.

"Yep," said Mom. "But I work with him a lot now that I'm a stylist, too."

Sydney didn't say anything, but I could tell from the look on her face that she was impressed. I was impressed too. Sometimes I forget that my mom knows famous designers.

"Okay, Mia," said Mom. "It's time for dinner."

I quickly got changed. When I got out, the PGC girls were still looking at clothes.

"See you around," I said, waving good-bye.

Mom and I left, and I felt a tiny bit guilty for having fun with Sydney and the girls from the PGC. I knew Katie, Alexis, and probably even Emma would think it was weird. But why should that matter? I could be friends with anyone I wanted to, *couldn't I*? It was all pretty confusing.

CHAPTER 6

The Same, Only Different

The next day at lunch, I didn't mention to Katie, Alexis, and Emma that I had run into the PGC girls at the mall. It wasn't like I was hiding anything. I just didn't want to make a big deal out of it.

Other than that, Thursday and Friday went by seriously slow, maybe because I knew that I'd be seeing my dad on Friday. I couldn't wait, and when I'm really excited about something, it feels like it takes forever to happen.

My mom picked me up at school and drove me to the train station. She always insists on parking the car and waiting with me on the platform until the train comes.

"Mom, I know how to get on a train," I told her. I say the same thing every time.

"Of course you do," Mom replied. "But I'm your mom, and I get to stay with you if I want to. That's one of the perks."

With a loud roar, the big silver commuter train came to a stop in front of us. I hoisted my purple duffel bag over my shoulder, and Mom gave me a huge hug and a kiss.

"Be good," she said. "Call me if you need me. I'll see you Sunday."

I climbed onto the train. The nice thing about being so far from the city is that I can always get a seat. The closer you get to Manhattan, the more crowded the train gets.

I found a window seat in the middle of the car and settled in, with my duffel bag across my lap. I waited until the conductor came and took my ticket, and then I got out my sketchbook and pushed in my earbuds. I listened to music and sketched for a while, but pretty soon I put down my pencil and just looked out the window. There are a lot of stops between my town and Manhattan, and sometimes I feel like I'll never get there.

It wasn't always this way. When my parents got divorced four years ago, their lawyers suggested they go to a judge to figure out who I would live with. They said it was the fairest way to decide. The judge said I should live with my mom full time and my dad every other weekend.

But when I lived in Manhattan, I saw my dad a lot more than that. I could always hop on a bus or a taxi and be at his apartment in less than twenty minutes. My mom used to work late at the magazine a lot, so I ended up hanging out with my dad a few nights a week.

That all changed in June when we moved in with Eddie and Dan. I hardly ever see my dad during the week anymore. The weekends I spend with him fly by. It just doesn't seem fair.

When the train finally pulled into Grand Central Station, I made sure to put my sketchbook back in my bag (I left one on the train once, which was seriously depressing) and made my way down the crowded car to the exit.

Dad was waiting for me on the platform, as usual. I ran up to him and gave him a big hug.

"Hey there, *mija!*" Dad said. (In case you didn't know, *mija* means "my daughter" in Spanish, and it's pronounced MEE-ha. Which is actually how I got my nickname, Mia. My full name is Amelia. But Dad kept saying *mija*, and Mom joked that it sounded like he was saying "Mia." And then Mia just stuck.)

"Hey," I said. "Where are we going for dinner tonight?"

"Hmm, I don't know," Dad said. "I was thinking . . . sushi?"

I smiled. Dad and I always have sushi on Friday nights. It's a good thing we both love it. So we made our way outside and took a cab to our favorite downtown sushi restaurant, Tokyo 16.

I love the taste of sushi—the cool fish, the salty seaweed, the dark taste of the soy sauce, and the spiciness of green wasabi paste, all in one bite. The other thing I like about sushi is that sushi restaurants are always beautiful. When you walk into Tokyo 16, the sounds of the city melt away behind you. There's a waterfall running on the back wall and the sound is very soothing. I love the shiny black chopsticks and the adorable tiny bowls that hold the soy sauce.

"So you and your friends won that contest last week," Dad said as we dug into our sushi rolls. "I'm really proud of you."

"Thanks," I replied. I dunked a roll of tuna and avocado wrapped in rice into the soy sauce. "We actually made two hundred cupcakes! I've never made that many cupcakes in my life."

"I bet they were really delicious," Dad said.

"You'll have to bring me one sometime."

I nodded yes because my mouth was full of sushi.

"I'm glad you're making new friends," Dad went on. "What are their names again?"

"Katie, Alexis, and Emma," I replied. "They're all nice." I thought about telling him about the PGC, but it was all kind of new.

"That reminds me," I said. "Ava invited me to her soccer game tomorrow morning and then out for pizza for lunch. Can I go?"

Dad made a pretend sad face. "You mean you don't want to spend all day with your dad?"

"You can pick me up in the afternoon," I told him. "Then we can do something."

"Actually, I made plans for us," Dad said. "My friend Alina is having an art opening. I think it would be fun to go."

I frowned. "Alina? Who is Alina?"

Dad cleared his throat. "We've been dating. She's really nice. You two are a lot alike. She's an amazing artist. It'll be fun."

I popped another piece of sushi into my mouth so I wouldn't have to say anything just yet. Dad had never talked to me about any of the women he dated before. Why was Alina different?

"It's our weekend together," I said. "Can't you

see her art show some other time?" I know I just told him that I was spending time with Ava, but that was different.

"It's opening night," Dad explained. "It's a big deal. There will be food and music and everything. You'll like it, I promise."

"Okay," I agreed. An art show sounded like fun, and Dad seemed really excited.

That night Dad and I watched a movie together before we went to sleep. The next morning, he took the subway with me to Ava's soccer game. He dropped me off with a wave, and I ran to meet Ava and her mom over by the bleachers. Ava was wearing a red and white soccer uniform with her team name, The Soho Slammers. Her straight dark hair was pulled back in a ponytail. Her mom was a few inches taller than Ava. She wore white leggings and a red T-shirt to match Ava's team colors.

"Mia, you are growing so big!" Mrs. Monroe said, hugging me. "What are they feeding you out in the suburbs?"

"Mystery meat loaf," I replied, and Ava burst into giggles.

"This is going to be an awesome game," Ava promised. "We're playing the girls from Riverside. Remember last year, we tied them?"

I nodded. Ava and I had played on the same soccer team since we were six years old. "You think you can beat them this year?"

Ava grinned. "I know we can!"

Ava's coach blew a whistle, and Ava ran off to join her team. I climbed up onto the bleachers with Mrs. Monroe.

It felt weird, sitting in the bleachers instead of being on the field. A big part of me really wished I was out there playing. But I couldn't because I didn't live in Manhattan anymore. I couldn't even play soccer in my new town, because I would have to miss every other game. It wasn't fair, but there was nothing I could do about it.

Mrs. Monroe and I cheered for the Slammers. Ava was right—it was an exciting game, and in the end, the Slammers won 3–2. We all went out for pizza after that, and I was with all my old friends again: Ava, Jenny with freckles, Tamisha, Madeline.

"Mia, we need you back on the team," Tamisha told me. "Nobody can make those long passes like you can."

"I wish," I said. "But you guys don't need me. You did great today."

Everyone let out a whoop. Then the talk turned from the game to gossip.

"Mia doesn't know yet," Ava announced.

"Know what?" I asked.

"Big news," Ava said. "Angelo got caught passing a note in class, and Mr. Tyler, our math teacher, read it out loud. You won't believe what it said!"

Everyone started laughing.

"Tell me! I can't stand the suspense!" I begged.

"It said that he has a crush on Madeline!" Ava shrieked, and everyone started laughing.

Madeline turned bright red. "The whole thing is seriously embarrassing," she said.

I started laughing really hard. Angelo thinks he's supercool. He's been slicking back his hair with gel since fifth grade. Poor Madeline.

I had a lot of fun at lunch. In a way, things were the same as always with me and my friends. But in another way, a big way, they were really different. I didn't get to beat Riverside. I wasn't there when Angelo got caught with the note.

It's a weird feeling—like I'm missing out on half of my life!

CHAPTER 7

The Friendship Police

*T*hat afternoon I dumped the contents of my purple duffel bag out on my Parisian Chic bedspread.

"I wish Dad had told me we were going to an art show before I packed," I muttered. He had said it was a big deal, but I didn't bring any "big deal" clothes with me—not even a single skirt. I kept rearranging the clothes I had and trying stuff on. Finally I decided on a pair of black leggings, a long white button-down shirt, and a cropped green cardigan over it.

I looked in the mirror. *Needs some sparkle,* I thought, so I added this cool vintage necklace with a green and blue crystal flower pendant that used to be my mom's.

When I went into the living room, Dad was busy putting on his tie. He looked really nice. My dad is tall, with jet-black hair and wire-rimmed glasses. He was wearing black pants, a black button-down shirt, a black tie, and black shoes. I don't like the all-one-color thing personally, but Dad can make it work.

"You look beautiful, *mija*. I've always loved that necklace," Dad told me. He glanced at his watch. "Let's go catch a cab."

"So what's Alina's art like?" I asked as we rode downtown.

"It's hard to describe. But you'll love it when you see it. I know you will," Dad promised.

The taxi pulled up in front of the gallery, which was on the first floor of a brick building. There were huge glass windows out front so you could see inside.

When Dad and I walked in, the first thing I noticed was the music. At least, I think it was music. It sounded like someone banging a stick against a metal garbage can over and over again while a remote control plane zipped through the air. It wasn't as loud as Dan's heavy metal, but it was just as annoying.

A tall, thin woman with short black hair walked

up to us. She was wearing all black—a sleeveless, short black dress, black tights, and black heels. That's when it hit me—she and Dad were dressed alike! Maybe this dating thing with Alina was more serious than I thought.

Alina gave my dad a hug and a kiss on each cheek. "Alex! You made it!" Then she smiled and held out her hand to me. "And this must be Mia. I'm Alina. It's nice to meet you."

"Nice to meet you, too," I said, to be polite. Inside, I wasn't sure yet.

"Your father tells me you're an artist," she said.

"Yes, she's always drawing in that sketchbook of hers," Dad said, patting my shoulder.

"Fashion designs, mostly," I told her. "I want to work in the fashion industry someday. Like my mom."

"The worlds of fashion and art are intertwined," Alina said. "Come, let me show you my work."

First she led us to a big white wall. There was a hole in the middle of it.

"I call this piece 'Rage,'" Alina said.

"It looks like someone punched a hole in the wall," I remarked.

"Exactly!" Alina looked really happy. "I encapsulated a moment of sheer rage and froze it in time."

"Hmm" was all I could manage.

But Dad was acting like it was the greatest thing in the world. "Brilliant, Alina. I love it!"

We moved to the next piece, a white canvas with some black blotches on it.

"This one is 'Rage, Part Two,'" Alina explained.

From what I could tell, she had gotten angry and thrown some paint against a canvas. But you won't believe what Dad said about it.

"Fascinating." He adjusted his glasses, like he was trying to see better. "You can feel the anger emanating from the piece."

The rest of the art was just like that. It was all weird, and Dad was acting like it was the best stuff in the world. I didn't say much, because I didn't want to hurt Alina's feelings.

When we were done looking at the art, some guy came up and whispered in Alina's ear.

"Got to go," she said. "A big art buyer walked in the door."

"Let's get some food," Dad suggested.

There was a food table in the back, but all they had were glasses of wine for the adults and some cucumber slices with pink glop on top. I was feeling pretty hungry, and the music was giving me a headache.

"So," Dad asked. "What do you think?"

"It's um, *interesting*," I said, and I realized I sounded like Sydney. "It's not really my style."

"That's art for you," Dad said. "Everyone has an opinion."

Luckily we didn't stay much longer, and Dad took pity on me and we picked up Chinese food on the way home. Later when I was sketching in my room, I started thinking about what Dad had said yesterday.

"You two are a lot alike."

I mean, seriously? First of all, I never wear all black—I leave that to the vampires like Bella. And I would never play music like that, and I *definitely* would not punch a hole in something and call it art. And when I have my first runway show, I plan on having a sushi buffet. Who wants to eat pink glop, anyway?

It was like Dad didn't really know me. The thought bothered me a lot.

As I stared at my pink and black walls, a thought crossed my mind that bothered me even more. When Mom and Eddie decided to get married, we moved in with Eddie. What if Dad and Alina got married? Would we move in with her?

I could just imagine her apartment—bare white

walls, all-black furniture, and that screechy music playing nonstop. I bet there are holes in the walls too.

I sank back into my pillows.

Don't panic, I told myself. *They're only dating.*

But I didn't sleep well that night at all.

Sunday was a pretty normal day with Dad—sleeping late, getting bagels, biking in the park, and Dad making his famous chicken in tomato sauce for a late lunch. Then it was the drive back home and sleep. My same old every-other-Sunday routine.

I woke up the next morning for school feeling really confused. First I was confused as always about where I was, then I kept thinking about Alina and Dad, and missing out on things with my friends from Manhattan. It took me forever to pick out an outfit for school. I kept wondering what an outfit would look like if you felt confused. Mixed patterns—plaid with stripes? I finally settled on some skinny jeans and a T-shirt with a graphic design of New York on it. It wasn't great, but it was the best I could come up with.

I was glad to see Katie on the bus.

"How was your weekend with your dad?" she asked.

"Pretty nice," I said. "Except he has this weird

girlfriend, Alina, who's an artist who punches things."

It felt good to talk about Alina out loud. I hadn't told my mom, of course. But talking to Katie is really easy—I feel like I can tell her anything.

Katie raised an eyebrow. "I hope she doesn't punch people."

"Only walls," I said. "And then she hangs it in a gallery."

"I'm glad my mom doesn't go on dates," Katie said. "That would be totally weird."

"It is totally, seriously weird," I assured her.

Braaaaaaap! Wes Kinney made what was probably his loudest fake burp yet. Katie and I shook our heads. Another Monday had begun.

After homeroom, my first class of the day is math, which is always painful even on non-Mondays. Bella and Callie are in that class too, so I waved when I came in and sat down.

Mrs. Moore hadn't arrived yet, so I took out my sketchbook and began to draw. I had been trying to come up with a sweater/skirt combo like the ones I'd seen in the magazine.

Callie sits behind me, and I noticed her looking over my shoulder. "That's really cute," she said. "I wish I could draw like that."

"You probably can," I told her. "I wasn't very good until I took lessons. Then I learned some ways to do things that I never thought of before."

"Can you show me sometime?" Callie asked.

I was about to answer her, but the bell rang just then. So I waited until after class. Callie and I both have science together second period, so I walked with her down the hallway.

"So Callie, if you want to draw together sometime, just let me know," I said.

"That would be nice," Callie replied. "I should give you my cell phone number. Come see me before you get on the bus and we can exchange, okay?"

"Okay," I said.

That's when I noticed Katie walking toward us. Her class was in the opposite direction.

"Hey!" I said with a wave. Katie waved but had a puzzled look on her face. I didn't understand why until I saw her later at lunch.

"So, what were you and Callie talking about?" Katie asked.

I thought it was kind of a strange question to ask. I mean, I can talk to whomever I want, can't I? For a moment I felt like I was being quizzed by the friendship police.

Then I remembered that Katie and Callie used to be *best* friends. So maybe Katie was just interested.

"Callie liked a drawing I did," I said. I left out the part about us maybe getting together. "I was sketching a sweater and a skirt."

Alexis rolled her eyes. "Is that all those PGC girls think about? Fashion and makeup?" she asked. "What about all of the problems in the world? Don't they know that the rain forest disappears bit by bit every day? And what about all those polar bears up north? All their ice is melting and they have nowhere to live! Doesn't the PGC care about that?"

Emma shook her head. "Alexis, you worry too much."

"You can't be serious *all* the time," I pointed out. "Besides, those PGC girls aren't all that bad."

"That's your opinion," Alexis said. "When I see them do something to help the polar bears, then maybe I'll change my mind."

Katie looked really worried and unhappy. I wasn't sure why. Maybe she was worried about the polar bears too. But I had a feeling that something else was bothering her—me.

CHAPTER 8

Sweet and Sour

The rest of the week was pretty normal, except that I spent every night cleaning the kitchen to get ready for the Cupcake Club meeting on Friday. Mostly it was Dan's mess. He is addicted to tortilla chips and cheese sauce, and so there are always piles of dried-up orange cheese all over the counters and the table. But if you try to talk to him about it, it goes like this:

Me: "Dan, can you please clean up that cheese all over the counter?"

Dan: "You mean that little orange dot?" (He takes a paper towel and moves it once over the cheese.) "Done."

But, of course, the cheese is still there.

I also had to figure out how to do the yellow and

green flowers for the top of each cupcake. I spent some time looking online. There are a lot of cool sites that sell cupcake and baking supplies.

Finally I found a site that sold these beautiful yellow flowers made out of sparkly sugar. Each flower had two little green leaves sticking out of it. They were so pretty! I showed them to Mom, and she ordered four dozen of them for me. She said we could pay her back after Ms. Biddle paid us.

Mom had a meeting in the city on Friday, and Dan had a basketball game, so Eddie got pizza for the two of us. I put Tiki and Milkshake up in my room because they go nuts when a lot of people come to the house.

Katie, Alexis, and Emma all showed up at seven. Emma's mom was standing behind them.

"I'll be back later to pick everyone up," she said. "What time do you think you'll be done?"

Katie spoke up. "If we can bake all four dozen at once, we'll probably be finished by nine," she said.

"Sounds good," Mrs. Taylor said. "I'll see you girls later."

Everyone came inside, and Eddie walked up with a big smile on his face.

"So, what kind of cupcakes are we making tonight?" he asked.

"*We* are making lemon cupcakes with cream cheese icing," I told him.

Eddie made a goofy frown. "Aw, don't I get to help?"

"You can be the official oven-turner-onner," Katie suggested.

"I can do that," Eddie said. "I'm an expert at that."

"We'll call you when we need you," I said. Then I nodded to my friends. "Follow me."

"Your stepdad is really funny," Emma remarked once we got inside the kitchen.

"*Almost* stepdad," I corrected her. "And you wouldn't say that if you spent more time with him. Most of his jokes are awful."

"Yeah, my dad thinks he's much funnier than he really is too," Emma said. "But I'd rather have that than some grumpy old dad."

Hmm, Emma had a point. I'd take Eddie's humor over Alina's anger issues any day!

Katie put the shopping bag she was carrying on the kitchen table, and Alexis took out her notebook.

"If we divide the tasks, we can get things done faster," she said. "Katie, since you're the best baker you can start mixing together the cupcake batter.

63

I'll squeeze the lemons for you. Emma, you can make the frosting. And Mia, you can work on the decorations for the cupcakes."

"It's going to be easy this time," I told her. I picked up the package of sugar flowers on the counter. "We just need to stick one on each cupcake, see?"

"Ooh, they're so pretty!" Emma said.

"Ms. Biddle's going to love them," Katie added.

"Okay, good," Alexis said. "Then Mia, you can help Katie with the batter. That should cover everything."

"Not everything," I said. I unclipped my iPod from the waistband of my skirt and plugged it into the player on the kitchen table. "We need some music."

I always work better with music in the background (unless it's Dan's heavy metal music), and pretty soon we were dancing around the kitchen as we worked. Katie and I measured out the flour, baking powder, and salt, and sifted them together. Then we melted some butter and put that in a bowl. We added some eggs, sugar, and vanilla. Alexis gave us a measuring cup with fresh lemon juice inside, and we dumped that into the rest of the wet ingredients. After we mixed those together, we slowly started adding the flour mixture. After doing two hundred cupcakes for the fund-raiser, we knew the steps pretty much by heart.

"Eddie! It's time to turn on the oven!" I called out.

Eddie came running into the kitchen like a football player running onto the field from the sidelines. "Okay, what temperature do we need?" he asked.

"Three hundred and fifty, please," Katie told him.

While the oven was heating up, we used an ice cream scoop to plop some batter into the lined cupcake pans. Katie had picked out yellow cupcake liners to match the flower on top. The batter was a pretty yellow color too.

"These are going to look so nice," Emma said as we slipped them into the oven.

I nodded. "Wait until we put the flowers and icing on top."

We set the timer for twenty minutes. That's one of the great things about cupcakes—they don't take long to cook. While the cupcakes baked, I washed the bowls we'd just used, and Katie dried them. Alexis took a spoon and took a taste of Emma's cream cheese frosting.

"Mmm, that is sooo good," she said. "It's going to go great with the lemon."

The timer buzzed, and Eddie came running into the kitchen.

"Better leave this to me, ladies," he said. "Hot stuff coming out!"

I rolled my eyes at Katie, and she smiled back. I knew she could appreciate how corny Eddie can be—she always says how corny her mom can be too.

Eddie removed the pans from the oven, and we showed him how to carefully tip over the pans onto the cooling racks. The cupcakes looked golden yellow and perfect, and they smelled super lemony.

We sat and talked while the cupcakes cooled off. Then I heard the front door bang shut. Dan was back.

"What's that smell?" he asked, walking into the kitchen. He was wearing his red and white basketball uniform, and he was pretty sweaty.

"Please do not get sweat on the cupcakes," I told him, and I heard Emma giggle behind me.

Dan ignored me. "I am so hungry. Mind if I take one?"

But he didn't wait for an answer. He just picked one up, broke it in half, and stuffed it in his mouth.

"Dan!" I shrieked. "Those are for a baby shower tomorrow. We're being *paid* to make those!"

Katie, Alexis, and Emma all looked as horrified as I felt.

"Maybe it's not so bad," Emma said. "We're only one short."

Then Dan made a face. "Whoa, what kind of cupcakes are these? They're supersour!"

"They're lemon cupcakes," Katie said. "They should taste like lemon, but also be sweet."

Dan handed the uneaten half of his cupcake back to me. "I don't know. It doesn't taste sweet to me."

"You just don't know a good cupcake when you taste one," I said. I broke off a piece and popped it into my mouth. The sour taste of lemon stung my tongue.

"Uh-oh," Katie said. "Is he right?"

I nodded. "It's really sour. Not sweet at all."

I handed each girl a piece of cupcake. Each one made a face as she tasted it.

"So, how much lemon did you put in these anyway?" Dan asked.

"I measured it myself," Alexis replied. "One and a half cups, just like the recipe said."

Katie frowned. "One and a half cups? I thought the recipe said one half cup."

"I don't think so. I'm pretty sure it was one and a half cups," Alexis said, but her voice didn't sound so sure.

Katie looked in the recipe book. "Nope. It says

right here, one half cup of lemon juice. That's probably what happened."

Alexis's face turned bright red. "Oh, no! I'm so sorry!"

I felt bad for her. "I should have checked when you handed me the measuring cup," I said. "It's my fault too."

"Looks like you guys need to make some more cupcakes," Dan said.

I looked at the clock. It was already after eight o'clock.

"I'll do it," Alexis said. "I'll stay up all night if I have to, but I'll finish them."

"Of course you won't," Emma said. "We're all in this together."

Katie grinned. "Don't sweat it, Alexis. You've got so many numbers in your brain, you were bound to get them mixed up sometime."

Alexis shook her head. "I still can't believe it. I thought I checked it, like, three times."

"You know, you guys should *thank* me for eating that cupcake," Dan told them. "Otherwise, whoever's paying you would have been pretty disappointed."

I hated to admit it, but Dan was right.

"You can be our official cupcake taster," Katie said.

"I don't know," Dan said. "It could be danger-ous."

Everybody laughed. Even though we had to start from scratch, it wasn't terrible, because we were all in it together, just like Emma said.

And that, unlike our cupcakes, was pretty sweet.

CHAPTER 9

Sadness at the Smoothie Shop

It was a night that would go down in cupcake history. First Katie, Alexis, and Emma had to call home to make sure they could stay late. Then we had to get to work on making the cupcakes from scratch again.

This time, we all watched closely as Katie measured each ingredient. After Alexis squeezed more lemons, she took the measuring cup to each of us to check it. It was exactly one half cup.

"Alexis, your flair for perfection has returned," Katie kidded her.

We filled the cupcake tins, stretching out the batter just a little bit so that we had two extra cupcakes with which we could do a taste test. Mom walked in just as we were putting the second batch in the oven. Even though she looked a little tired, she still looked fabulous. She wore a ruffled ivory shirt with sleek trousers, a gold necklace and bangle bracelets, and, of course, her favorite black high heels.

"Eddie says you had a cupcake emergency," she said. "Anything I can do to help?"

"We've got it under control," I told her. "When the cupcakes are done, we'll wait until they cool, then ice them and decorate them."

I noticed that Alexis was standing six inches from the oven, staring through the glass window that showed the cupcakes baking inside.

"Alexis, what are you doing?" I asked.

"Making sure they don't burn," she said. "We don't have time to make a new batch if this goes wrong."

"Whoa, I didn't think of that," Katie said. She stood next to Alexis and peered through the window.

"Seriously, you can't look through that thing for twenty minutes, can you?" I asked.

"Oh yes we can," Katie replied.

"Well, I'm going to do the dishes," I replied.

Emma grabbed a dishtowel. "I'll help."

Katie and Alexis stayed glued to the oven until the timer went off. Eddie came in to take them out again.

71

"You know what they say. Second time's the charm!" he said cheerfully.

"Where's Dan?" Katie asked. "We need our official cupcake taster."

"In the family room, watching TV," Eddie replied.

Katie ran out of the kitchen and came back a minute later, dragging Dan by the arm.

"I don't know if I want this job," he said. "It's risky."

"Very funny," I said. I handed him a cupcake. "Now taste."

Dan took a bite. He made a face, just like before.

"Oh, no!" Alexis wailed. "Is the cupcake sour again?"

We were all staring at him. Even Eddie looked nervous.

Dan smiled. "JK! No. It's good." We all sighed with relief. Dan hung out in the kitchen a little bit watching us with Eddie, but he didn't get in our way. I think it's the first time there were ever that many girls in their kitchen. I wondered if it was a little weird for them.

But we still weren't finished. By the time we let the cupcakes cool, iced them, and added the flowers, it was almost eleven thirty. Yawning, we began to put the cupcakes in the special boxes we had.

Emma's mom walked into the kitchen with my mom. They were both yawning too.

"Are you girls ready to go?" Mrs. Taylor asked.

I snapped the lid on the fourth cupcake box. "All done."

"I'll drive tomorrow," my mom told Emma's mom. "We'll be by to get Emma around eleven."

"I'll be at Emma's house," Alexis said.

"Thanks for letting us use your kitchen, Ms. Vélaz," Katie said.

"No problem," my mom told her. "Now go home and get a good night's sleep!"

The girls left, but I still had one thing to do before I went to bed. I wrote "DO NOT EAT" on a piece of paper and taped it to the cupcake boxes. Dan might have helped us out, but I still didn't trust him.

Luckily, Dan didn't touch the cupcakes, and they were beautiful and perfect when we dropped them off at Ms. Biddle's house the next morning.

I'd never been to a teacher's house before. I was kind of expecting her to live in a mad scientist's lab, with test tubes bubbling over or something. But she lived in a cute little red house with no test tubes in sight. A fat orange cat was lazing in the sunny window when we rang the bell.

Ms. Biddle was happy to see us. She wasn't wearing a crazy science shirt. Instead, she had on a yellow button-down shirt and linen capris. Today Ms. Biddle's outfit said to me that she was happy and calm. Yellow is known to be a very happy color.

"Wow, you guys are professional," she said. "Come on in."

The living room and the dining room were decorated with pale yellow and green streamers and matching balloons. She pointed to a skinny table in the dining room with a pile of yellow plastic plates on it.

"I thought we could put the cupcakes here," she said.

"Perfect!" I said. "We'll set them up so they look nice."

We arranged all of the cupcakes on the yellow plates and lined them up on the table. It all looked really pretty.

"My sister's going to love this," Ms. Biddle said. "Thanks so much."

She held out a white envelope, and Alexis reached for it. "I'll take that," she said. "Thanks a lot."

We waited until we were back outside, and we gave one another a high five.

"We did it!" Katie cheered. "Our first paying job!"

"I'm really proud of all of you," my mom said. "Let's go to Sal's Smoothies. My treat."

Fifteen minutes later we were sitting in a booth at Sal's. It's a fun place, with pink walls and lime green cushions in the booths. We each got a different flavor. Katie got banana berry, Alexis got ginger and peach, Emma got strawberry, and I got mango with passionfruit.

Alexis opened up the envelope and counted out the money. "Forty-eight dollars," she announced. "One dollar per cupcake."

"We still need to pay back my mom," Katie said. She dug into her pocket and handed a crumpled receipt to Alexis. "All the ingredients came to sixteen dollars, but we can use the leftover flour and sugar the next time we bake."

Then I remembered about the sugar flowers. "Mom, do you have the receipt for that?" I asked.

"I think so," Mom replied. She searched through her purse and came up with a piece of white paper. She handed it to Alexis.

Alexis slurped on her smoothie as she studied it. "No way," she said. "Those flowers were seventy-five cents a piece?"

"Um, I guess so," I said. "I thought that was pretty reasonable. Seventy five cents isn't a lot of money."

"But seventy-five cents times forty-eight is thirty-six dollars," Alexis said. "That means we spent fifty-two dollars making these cupcakes— that's four dollars over budget!"

I felt awful. "I'm sorry, really."

"Don't worry about the flowers," Mom said quickly. "Think of it as a donation for your start-up business. We businesswomen need to stick together."

"That's really nice of you," Emma said.

Alexis was shaking her head. "This is why we need to do a budget every time. We can't make mistakes like this."

"It's our first paying job, remember," Katie said. "We're going to make lots of mistakes starting out. Like putting in too much lemon juice."

Alexis blushed. "You're right. I didn't mean to get upset. Thanks, Ms. Vélaz."

"I think we should save the money we made and use it for our next order," Katie said. "Then we won't spend any more than we have."

"That sounds like something Alexis would say," Emma kidded her.

Katie grinned. "What can I say? She must be rubbing off on me."

"I'm sorry, Mia. I didn't mean to make you feel bad," Alexis said.

"It's okay," I said.

After that, nobody talked about the cost of the flowers again. But I still felt really bad. I didn't say much after that, and I didn't even finish my smoothie.

CHAPTER 10

An Invitation

$\mathcal{M}$om, can we go to the mall?" I asked. We had just dropped off the girls and were heading home, but I needed a serious mall experience.

"Why not?" Mom asked. "I need a new charger for my cell phone anyway."

Soon we were walking through the doors of the Westgrove Mall. "Are you going to Icon again?" Mom asked.

"I was thinking Blue Basics," I said. It's a great shop that sells every kind of jeans you can think of, plus classic shirts and sweaters. I love jeans because everything goes with them. Plus I grew, like, a foot over the summer, so all of mine were too short.

Mom must have been reading my mind. "Good

idea. You need some new jeans anyway. I'll meet you there in a little bit. Cell phone on?"

"And charged," I told her.

Mom turned the corner, and I headed to Blue Basics, which is on the first floor. I hadn't gotten far when I saw Sydney, Maggie, Bella, and Callie walking toward me.

"Hi!" I said.

"Wow, I can't believe we ran into you again!" Maggie gushed.

"It's like destiny," Bella said in a serious voice.

"Or maybe it's just that we all like to look at clothes," Callie pointed out.

I smiled. "I don't know. I think fashion is my destiny, sometimes."

"Well of course it is, with a famous mother like that." Maggie brushed a stray lock of frizzy hair out of her face. "It's in your blood."

"She's not famous, exactly," I replied.

"But she knows famous designers!" Maggie said. "I still can't believe she knows Damien Francis. Have you ever been to his house?"

"It's not like that," I tried to explain, but I don't think Maggie was interested in the boring truth. So I changed the subject. "I'm going to Blue Basics. Do you guys want to come?"

"Ooh, the Double B!" Maggie said. "I could use some new jeans."

Then Sydney spoke up for the first time. "We'll go with you," she said, and I got the feeling that the decision was hers to make.

Sydney walked beside me as we made our way to the store. "Maggie can get soooo starstruck," she said. "Once she spent a whole day outside Dave's Pizza in Manhattan because she heard that Justin Bieber liked to eat there when he came to New York."

"That was such a lie!" Maggie said with a pout. "But at least the pizza was really good."

"So, does your mom know any other designers?" Sydney asked casually.

"She knows a lot of them," I said truthfully. "She was in charge of choosing the clothes for the magazine's photo shoots. So any designer who wanted to get into *Flair* had to get friendly with my mom."

"So you must get a lot of free clothing samples, then," she said.

I shrugged. "Sometimes."

"But your mom doesn't work at *Flair* anymore?" Sydney asked.

"No, she started her own consulting business," I replied. "So she's still in fashion."

Sydney was being nice, but I was starting to feel like I was being interviewed or something.

Thankfully, the questions stopped once we got to Blue Basics. We must have spent an hour trying on different pairs of jeans. I was really glad the PGC girls were there because they stopped me from buying a pair of bleached-out jeans that were too "eighties," even for me. I ended up with two pairs of skinny jeans that my mom paid for when she got there.

Before I left, Sydney came up to me. "So, Mia, why don't you eat lunch with us on Monday?"

I hesitated. "Um, I don't know. I have friends that I sit with already."

"Your cupcake crew won't miss you for one day," Sydney said.

"Come on, Mia," Callie urged. "Let us share you with your other friends."

I liked the way Callie put it. I wasn't ditching the Cupcake Club, just sharing my time with other friends I liked. There was nothing wrong with that. It was just one lunch, after all.

"Okay," I said. "I'll see you on Monday."

Mom and I each got a big salad from the make-your-own-salad place on the way out of the mall. When we got home, I was anxious to try on my new jeans and plan some new outfits with them.

"Mom, where's my white button-down shirt?" I asked, after I'd finished petting Milkshake and Tiki.

"I thought I saw it in the laundry basket," Mom replied.

"Oh, right." I headed for the laundry room, which is right next to the kitchen. But the laundry basket was empty.

"Mom! It's empty!" I called out.

Eddie poked his head into the laundry room. "Dan did a wash this morning. Check the dryer."

I opened up the dryer and saw a bunch of colored clothes. I started to panic. Dan wouldn't have put my white shirt in with the colors, would he?

But that's exactly what he did. I pulled out my white button-down shirt, only it wasn't white anymore. Now it was streaked with pink.

"It's ruined!" I wailed.

I stomped into the kitchen where Mom and Eddie were sitting and drinking coffee. "Look at this! It's ruined! It's all Dan's fault!"

Usually I can stay pretty cool when something goes wrong. But for some reason, the ruined shirt was making me furious.

"Calm down," Mom said. "Dan didn't mean to ruin it, Mia."

"I'll buy you another shirt," Eddie added.

"That's not the point!" I fumed. "This *never* happened when it was just you and me, Mom. Why can't things just be the way they were?"

"Oh, Mia," Mom said sadly.

I felt like I was going to cry, so I ran up to my room. Tiki and Milkshake were so scared of me that they hurried out of my path. When I got to my room, I slammed the door shut behind me. Then I flopped onto my bed and put a pillow over my head.

I wished we had never left Manhattan. I wished Mom had never met Eddie. I wished a lot of things were different.

I also knew that my wishes didn't mean anything, and that's what hurt the most.

CHAPTER 11

I Finally Get It

 A few minutes later, Mom knocked on my door. "Come in," I said.

I quickly wiped away my tears and sat up as Mom walked in.

"Mia, can we talk?" Mom asked. "I understand that you're upset. Honestly I do. I also know that there's a lot more than a pink shirt that's bothering you."

I nodded. "Living here is hard sometimes."

"I know it's a big change," Mom said. "For all of us, really. But Eddie and I are trying really hard to make it good for you here. And you know I wanted to move away from Manhattan even before I met Eddie. I love Manhattan, but it's too fast there. I needed to slow down, you know?"

I nodded. "I know."

"And I thought you liked Eddie?" Mom asked. "You were the one who told me I should keep dating him."

I realized that was true. When Mom first introduced me to Eddie, I thought he was supernice. He still is.

"I do like him," I said. "But I miss Manhattan. I miss my friends. I miss being close to Dad."

I started to cry again. I couldn't help it. It was like the floodgates had opened and everything kept pouring out.

"I feel like an alien here sometimes. Even my room doesn't feel like me—I mean look at this room!" I said.

Mom was quiet for a minute and looked around my room. It was like she was looking at it for the first time.

"I guess I've been so busy lately I hadn't noticed. I'm sorry," Mom said. "You're right, this room is kind of depressing. Wow, look at that wallpaper. . . . I bet Eddie picked it out."

We both started to laugh. Mom hugged me and we sat there laughing about the room for a bit.

"Here's the thing," she said finally. "I love Eddie, and I think being here is a good place for us. But

I'll do what I can to make things easier, okay? For example, I'll get you your own laundry basket with your name on it. Then you can do your own laundry just the way you like it. And we'll redo your room over the next few weeks."

"That sounds good," I said.

"And *maybe* when I have meetings in the city in the afternoons, you can come along," Mom said. "You could have dinner with your dad or see your friends. But only if you have little or no homework!"

"Oh yes, yes! Thanks, Mom!" I squealed with delight.

Mom kissed me on the head. "I love you, Mia."

"I love you too, Mom."

"And Mia?" Mom said. "It's a little hard for Dan, too. Just try to remember that, okay?"

I thought about Dan watching us in the kitchen. It was just Dan and Eddie before we moved in. Just like it was just Mom and me before.

"Okay," I said.

I felt better after that. But I had one more thing to worry about. I would have to tell Katie, Alexis, and Emma that I wasn't eating lunch with them. And I really did not want to do that. Of course, I had to do it on a Monday.

I tried to tell Katie on the bus ride, but I chickened out. Then I tried to tell Alexis in the hallway, but I chickened out again.

Then it was time for lunch. I had no choice. I *had* to tell them. I walked up to our usual table before Alexis and Emma got in the lunch line.

"Hey," I said. "Um, listen, guys, today I'm sitting with Sydney and Callie and those guys. Just for today."

A hurt look crossed Katie's face, and I felt terrible.

"You mean the PGC?" Alexis asked. "Why on earth would you sit with them?"

"It's just—we keep meeting at the mall, and we like to talk about fashion and stuff," I said. "They invited me to eat with them today, and I didn't want to be rude or anything."

"If you want to talk about sweaters and skirts for forty minutes, then be my guest," Alexis said.

"Yeah, have fun," Emma said.

"It's cool," Katie said, but I could tell it was definitely not cool with her.

"Okay then. See you in English class," I said.

When I got to the PGC table, there was an empty seat between Callie and Maggie. I sat down.

"So, did the cupcake crew give you clearance to sit with us?" Sydney asked.

"It's not like that," I said. "I mean, I can sit where I want."

"I'm glad you're sitting with us," Callie said. "You know, my sister, Jenna, has known your stepbrother since kindergarten. She says he's really cute and nice."

"She must be confusing him with someone else," I said. "I mean, I guess he's cute. And he can be nice sometimes. But mostly he's seriously annoying."

"So is Jenna," Callie said. "No wonder they get along!"

Sydney rolled her eyes. "I'm an only child, thank goodness!"

"You can have my little sisters if you want," Maggie chimed in. "They drive me crazy!"

"I wouldn't mind having a brother or a sister," Bella said. "Sometimes it can be really lonely being an only child."

"Bella, you have said some ridiculous things before, but that might be the most ridiculous," Sydney told her, and I quickly looked at Bella. Were her feelings hurt?

But it didn't seem to faze her. "One day someone will recognize the beauty of my lonely soul," Bella said. "Until then, I will suffer alone."

Callie laughed. "Bella, you need to go to drama school, seriously."

"So, did anyone else take Mrs. Moore's quiz today?" Maggie asked. "It was superhard, I swear!"

"Oh, great," Callie moaned. "Not another one!"

"I've got a better one," Sydney said. "Did anyone see that outfit Sophie's wearing today? A plaid skirt and a top with a matching plaid collar? It looks like she's wearing a school uniform or something."

I happen to like Sophie a lot, so I wasn't happy with Sydney's comment.

"I loved the skirt," I said. "Maybe the top isn't a great match, but she's got the right idea."

"Yeah," Callie agreed. "She definitely gets points for that skirt. It's adorable."

Sydney just rolled her eyes.

The rest of the lunch went kind of like that. Maggie chattered on a mile a minute. Bella occasionally said something weird and dramatic. Sydney made slightly mean comments, and Callie and I had a completely normal conversation.

I wonder what Callie's doing with the rest of these girls? I found myself thinking. *She's really friendly and cool.*

Then it hit me. That's what Katie had been upset about since the first day of school. I tried to imagine if Ava stopped hanging out with me and hung out with other girls instead. It would be totally weird, and I wouldn't like it one bit. And now here I was doing kind of the same thing Callie had.

Katie wasn't trying to be the friendship police. She just didn't want to lose another friend. (You probably figured that out already, but what can I say? I really didn't get it until just then.)

When the bell rang, I walked up to Katie as she was leaving the cafeteria.

"How was your lunch?" she asked, and I noticed that she wasn't looking directly at me.

"Fine," I said. "But you know, it wasn't a permanent thing or anything. Tomorrow it's back to normal."

"Cool," Katie said.

I'm not sure if that made her feel any better, but I hope it did. Katie was one of the nicest things about Park Street School, and I didn't want to lose her as a friend.

CHAPTER 12

Not a Good Mix

At dinner that night it was Mom, Eddie, Dan, and me all at the same time. That doesn't happen a lot because of Eddie's work or Mom's meetings or Dan's basketball. I still felt a little bad about my freak-out in front of Eddie, but he hadn't said anything to me about it.

Eddie, as usual, was in a happy mood.

"Mmm, this is delicious, Sara," he said, swallowing a bite of food. "What is this called again?"

"Chicken *piccata*," Mom replied. "*Piccata* means 'larded' in Italian but there's no lard in this, just a sauce of butter and lemon juice."

"What are these little hard round things?" Dan asked.

"Capers," Mom said. "It's a pickled flower bud."

"They taste kind of weird," Dan said. "But the chicken's really good."

"I always pick the capers out," I said, and then it hit me—I was agreeing with Dan. Double weird!

"Well, I love it, capers and all," Eddie said, taking another bite.

Mom put down her fork and smiled at us. "So, I have some good news. I'm going to hold a fashion show to launch my new business. Right here in town!"

"That's wonderful news, honey!" Eddie said. "When will it be?"

"Two weeks," Mom said. "Yes, I know that's not a lot of time. But I made friends with a woman who owns the big banquet hall downtown, and they have an opening, and the space is terrific. . . . I couldn't resist."

"I'll help!" I offered.

"I was hoping you would," Mom said. "Especially backstage, styling the models. But I'll also need help from the Cupcake Club."

"Really?"

"Really," Mom said. "The show's going to be on a Sunday, so you'll have all Saturday to bake. And you'll need it. I'm going to need eight dozen cupcakes."

"If we bake them here, we can do four dozen at a time," I said, thinking quickly. "So that's about four to six hours together. We could do that in a day."

"Nice math, Mia!" said Eddie, and I smiled. Eddie sometimes had to help me with my math homework.

"The whole theme is going to be how to spice up your look with key pieces and accessories," Mom said. "So maybe you can use that idea for your cupcakes somehow. I'll pay you for the ingredients plus a dollar per cupcake. How does that sound?"

"I've got to tell everyone, but I'm sure it'll be okay," I said. I was starting to feel excited. "This is going to be really fun."

After dinner I grabbed my cell phone and texted Katie, Emma, and Alexis at the same time.

Mom's got a big job for us! Must talk at lunch tomorrow.

Yay! Katie replied.

Can't wait! texted Emma.

I hope she doesn't want lemon lol, was Alexis's response.

Another text came in. I figured it was from someone in the Cupcake Club, but it was Sydney.

Lunch 2morrow?

Can't, I texted back. Maybe next time. Thanks
though!

I knew that probably meant I'd never be asked to
sit with the PGC again, but I couldn't worry about
that now. The Cupcake Club had a lot of planning
to do!

The next day at lunch we got down to business.
Alexis had her notebook, of course, and Katie had
brought a book full of cupcake recipes.

I told them what details I knew—how much
Mom was paying us, how we'd have a whole
Saturday to do it, and about the whole "spice up
your wardrobe" theme.

"There are lots of recipes for spiced cupcakes
in here," Katie said, flipping through the recipe
book. "Like zucchini spice cupcakes, and chocolate spice cupcakes, and tea spice cupcakes, and
applesauce . . ."

"How can we pick just one?" Emma wondered
aloud.

"Maybe we don't have to," Alexis said. "We're
baking two batches of cupcakes anyway. We might
as well bake two different flavors."

"That's a great idea," I said. "That way if somebody doesn't like one flavor, they can choose a different one."

Alexis looked at her notebook and frowned. "We have so much to do. We have to figure out what we're making and make an ingredients list and figure out how to decorate."

"We probably need to think of how to display them too," I said. "This is going to be a pretty classy event. We can't just put the cupcakes out on paper plates."

Katie looked excited. "I saw a cupcake show on TV where they made cupcakes for a party at an amusement park, and the display looked like a roller coaster with all these cupcakes on it."

"So you think we should make a roller coaster?" Alexis asked.

"Of course not," Katie said. "But I bet we could come up with something just as awesome."

"We should meet this weekend," I said, and then I remembered. "Oh wait, I can't. I'm going to Dad's this weekend."

"How about after school?" Katie suggested. "Mom gets home early on Wednesdays. We could do it at my house."

"That would be great," I said, and Alexis and Emma agreed.

After lunch, Callie came up to me in the hallway.

"Hey, we're going to the mall after school," she said. "Maggie's mom is driving us. Do you want to come?"

"Sure," I said. "I need to get there soon anyway. My mom's doing a big fashion show in a few weeks, and I'm going to help style the models."

I hadn't told Katie and the others this part of it all, but I was really excited to talk to Callie.

"Oh, wow, that sounds really awesome," Callie said. "I've never been to a fashion show before. I've always wanted to go to one. I bet Sydney would love to go too."

I was about to blurt out to Callie that she and the PGC could come, but I stopped myself. It was Mom's show for her business, and I didn't know if she had any extra tickets or not. Besides, even though it was a fashion show, it was still a Cupcake Club thing, you know? And one thing I've figured out is that the PGC and the Cupcake Club are not a good mix.

"Yeah, it's really amazing to see them in person," I said. I didn't want to promise Callie anything just yet.

I had some thinking to do.

CHAPTER 13

General Sydney

After school I texted Mom and asked if I could go to the mall with Callie and the others. She made me get the number of Maggie's mom so she could make sure an adult was going with us. But then she said it was okay.

I realized I was a little bit nervous when Maggie's mom pulled up in her blue minivan. Before, I'd only met the PGC at the mall by accident. But now I was going with them, as part of the group. I've never felt nervous about going out with friends before in my life. So why was this different?

We climbed into the van. Maggie sat in front with her mom, Sydney and Bella took the second row, and Callie and I sat in the last row. I didn't see a crumb or speck of dirt anywhere, and everything smelled like vanilla.

Maggie's mom had brown hair, like Maggie, but hers was superstraight. She wore a large pair of sunglasses that were half as big as her face. I know all the celebrities wear those big sunglasses, but whenever I see them on someone it always makes me think of bugs.

"Mia, I spoke to your mother on the phone," Mrs. Rodriguez said, looking in the rearview mirror so she could see me. "What a lovely woman."

"Thanks," I said.

Callie leaned forward. "Mia's mom is holding a fashion show for her new business! Can you believe it?"

Maggie turned around so fast, I thought her head might fly off. "Oooh, a real fashion show! When is it? Where is it? Will Damien Francis be there?"

"It's in two weeks, at the banquet hall downtown," I replied. "I'm not sure who's going to be there yet. It's all happening so fast."

Maggie, Bella, and Callie started chattering with excitement.

"I wonder what kind of clothes the models will be wearing," Bella wondered.

"And where is she getting the models? From

here in town?" Maggie asked. "Ooh, maybe there'll be a model competition."

"I'd love to take photos during the show," Callie said.

Sydney was the only one who remained cool about it. But when the talking died down, she turned and looked right at me.

"Of course we can go with you, right?"

And of course, I didn't know what to tell her. "Um, I'm not sure," I said. "I'm going to be backstage helping Mom, so . . ."

"But she must have extra tickets she can give out." Sydney wasn't giving up. "We could go, even if you're backstage."

"I have to ask her," I said honestly. "I don't know how many tickets she has."

"Well, it all sounds very exciting," Maggie's mom said as we pulled into the mall. "Now, let's meet back up at five o'clock. Where should we meet?"

"We'll be at the smoothie place at five," said Sydney. I thought it was kind of interesting that Sydney was the one who answered, not Maggie.

"We have to go to Forever Young first," Sydney said as we walked through the door. "I saw some dresses on their website that I just have to try on."

That sounded good to me. The clothes in Forever

Young are really cute. They blast really loud dance music, though, so it's hard to have a conversation.

After about twenty minutes in there I was ready to leave. But Sydney tried on dress after dress after dress. I noticed that Maggie and Bella always said the same things each time.

"That one's fabulous!"

"You look sooooooo cute!"

"You *have* to get that."

Callie and I were definitely more honest. For example, I thought the blue dress with the bubble skirt was way too short, so I said so.

Sydney looked in the mirror. "Wow, you're right, Mia."

"That *is* way too short," Maggie quickly agreed.

"Definitely," Bella added.

We finally left Forever Young. Then we went up to the second floor and I saw the sign for Icon, which, as you know, is my favorite store there.

"I think they've got new jackets," I said, heading for the door.

Sydney grabbed my arm. "We can't go in there. It's Tuesday."

I was puzzled. "So?"

"Tuesday is the day that this salesgirl named Denise works there," Maggie explained for Sydney.

"She is, like, so totally rude. Once Sydney wanted to take ten items into the dressing room, and she was like, 'Sorry, it's store policy.' Can you imagine? Like, what's the big deal?"

"Oh," I said. "Okay. Fine." But it seemed like a silly reason not to go into the store.

"We're going to Monica's next," Sydney said. Then she marched off toward the store without waiting to hear if anyone else liked the idea. We all followed right behind her. For a second I got an image in my mind of Sydney in an army general's uniform, leading the troops.

Monica's is this store that sells accessories, like jewelry, hair bands and barrettes, bags, and stuff like that. I was actually happy we were there because I could get some ideas for the fashion show.

I found this cute red beret and clipped a rhinestone pin to it. I gave it to Callie.

"Here, put this on. I want to take a picture."

Callie put it on. "Hold on. I'll give you my supermodel look."

She tilted her head and got this totally fierce look on her face, just like a model in a magazine. I laughed.

"Perfect!" I snapped some photos with my cell phone.

I started looking at the necklaces next. I saw some cool-looking chokers and some really long chains with different stones linked in. I started wondering how the chokers and the long chains would look together, so I ran up to Maggie and draped them around her neck.

"Ooh, that's pretty!" Maggie said.

"Okay, hold still," I told her. Maggie smiled as I snapped a few more pictures.

I was really having fun. I was looking through the handbags when Sydney spoke up in a loud voice.

"I am so done here. Let's go to Basic Blue."

"Could we stay a little bit longer?" I asked.

Sydney was firm. "Maggie's mom is picking us up at five, remember? I don't want to spend all our time in one place."

But it's only been fifteen minutes! I wanted to say. *And you spent, like, an hour in Forever Young!* But somehow I knew it was useless to argue with Sydney.

So we all went to Blue Basics, and I was bored because I was just there on Saturday. This time, Callie and I hung out and talked while Maggie and Bella oohed and ahhed over Sydney's outfits. I found out that she has an older brother in college and that she became friends with the PGC when she went to summer camp. I told her all about Ava and my dad's apartment in New York. She's really easy to talk to.

Then Sydney appeared in front of us. "We're going to Sal's Smoothies," she informed us.

Sal's Smoothies is pretty popular in this town—there's a store downtown and one in the mall, too. We got in line to place our orders.

"We will have five ginger peach smoothies," Sydney told the girl at the counter.

Five? "Can you make mine a mango and passion fruit instead, please?" I asked the counter girl.

Sydney looked at me. "We always order ginger peach."

"I like ginger on my sushi," I said. "But not in my smoothie. It's weird."

"So, four ginger peach and one mango passion?" the girl asked.

Sydney didn't answer.

"Yes," I said.

I was kind of quiet when we sat down to drink our smoothies. To be honest, Sydney's bossiness was really getting to me.

I started thinking about my other friends in the Cupcake Club. Alexis can be a bit bossy, I guess, but she's just trying to organize complicated things, like schedules and budgets. And she's never mean. Then there's Katie. When it comes to recipes and stuff, she's usually the one to come up with ideas first. So she's like a leader in that way. But she's always interested in hearing everyone else's ideas too.

I tried to imagine Katie in a general's uniform, ordering everyone around the kitchen—"Crack those eggs now! Measure that milk! Sift that flour!"—but I couldn't.

Sydney, on the other hand . . . well, that was how she was. Mom always says that you can't expect people to change. You either accept how they are or stay away.

I wasn't sure how I was feeling, exactly. I liked hanging out with the PGC, especially Callie, and trying on clothes and talking about fashion. I absolutely didn't like Sydney's bossiness. Why do things always have to be so complicated?

CHAPTER 14

A Spicy Afternoon

$\mathcal{T}$he next day after school I had a completely different experience. I got off the bus with Katie for the Cupcake Club meeting. Katie lives in a small white house. There are orange flowers planted in pots on either side of the front door. When we got inside, Katie's mom called to us from the kitchen.

"Hello!" she said cheerfully. "How was school today?"

"Good," Katie answered. "Unless you count Mrs. Moore's daily quiz of death."

Mrs. Brown was shaking her head when we walked into the kitchen. "She can't be that bad, can she?"

"Oh yes, she can," Katie said. "Right, Mia?"

"True," I agreed. "But she did buy a cupcake from

us at the fund-raiser, so maybe she's not *all* bad."

Katie sighed. "Maybe not."

"So I picked up all the ingredients for your first test run," said Mrs. Brown. She kind of looks like Katie. They have the same big brown eyes and brown hair, only Katie's is long and Mrs. Brown's is shoulder length. Mrs. Brown is always either wearing her dental smock or an apron. So trying to guess what she's into isn't that hard. "I like your idea of doing spiced cupcakes. Very clever," she said.

Katie's kitchen table was loaded with everything we needed to make the cupcakes. Her kitchen looks really fun all the time. The walls are yellow, and there's this really cute cookie jar shaped like an apple and salt and pepper shakers that look like two blue birds in a nest.

The doorbell rang, and Katie ran to get it. She came back in followed by Alexis and Emma.

"Wow, we have a lot to do," Alexis said, looking at all the ingredients. "I still need to work out the budget for everything, and we need to think of a display."

"You can do the budget while we mix," Katie suggested. "And we can talk about the display while the cupcakes are cooling."

"That sounds good!" Alexis agreed. She sat down

at the table and opened up her notebook.

Katie, Emma, and I got to work on the apple-sauce spice cupcakes, which we'd decided to test first. We used applesauce, cinnamon, and nutmeg in the batter, and the kitchen quickly began to smell fabulous. Alexis had finished her budget by the time the cupcakes were in the oven, so we had a chance to talk while we did the dishes and worked on the frosting.

"Mia, do you think you can decorate the cup-cakes for twenty-five cents apiece?" Alexis asked me.

"Sure," I said. "I've been looking at a bunch of different things online, and they're all cheaper than the sugar flowers."

"Great," Alexis said. "Then we should make a profit this time."

I winced a little bit and looked at Alexis, but she was scribbling numbers. Did she mean that as a jab at my last mess up?

"Cool," Katie said. "Now we just have to figure out how to display them."

"I was thinking about that," I said. "It might be cool to have something that's raised above the table, so people can really see them from a distance. They'll be easier to pick up, too."

I walked over to the table. "Alexis, can I borrow a page in your notebook?"

Alexis nodded, and I started to sketch my idea: a pole with a round plate on the bottom, another plate about ten inches above that one, and a third plate about another foot higher.

Katie, Alexis, and Emma gathered around while I sketched.

"Very cool," Katie said. "I bet we'd need two of them to hold all eight dozen cupcakes."

"They are cool," Alexis agreed. "But how will we make them?"

"My dad and I make stuff all the time," Emma spoke up. "He's got lots of spare wood in the garage, and I know we have wooden poles we could use."

"That would be awesome!" I said. "I was thinking we could paint them red, but I'll check with my mom tonight and let you know at lunch tomorrow."

"That reminds me," Alexis said. "I never asked how your lunch went with the PGC. Did Sydney spend the whole time insulting everyone in school?"

I thought about what Sydney had said about Sophie. "Well, not everyone," I replied. "But mostly we talked about normal stuff. Like Mrs. Moore's math quizzes. And brothers and sisters. It wasn't so different from stuff we talk about."

"Right. Because we are *so* much alike," Alexis said sarcastically. "I'll believe that when Emma comes to school dressed like a vampire, and Katie dyes her hair blond."

"Now you're starting to sound like Sydney," Emma said.

Alexis blushed. "Sorry. Those girls bug me, that's all. I survived three years of their torture at summer camp. It's hard to get over."

"I don't think being blond is Sydney's problem," I added.

"Right. Your hair color has nothing to do with your personality," said blond-haired Emma.

"All right, all right, I'll drop it," Alexis said. "Isn't it time to frost these cupcakes now?"

We started putting the vanilla cinnamon frosting on the cupcakes. We spread the frosting on with a special knife Mrs. Brown uses. It makes the icing look smooth and shiny.

"You know, I was thinking," I said. "I've seen it in some of Katie's books—how you put the icing in a pastry bag and then pipe it out onto the top of the cupcake. You can do swirls or little dots, stuff like that."

"Mom has pastry bags," Katie said quickly. She ran into her big pantry and came out with plastic bags shaped like triangles and two metal tips. Then she showed us how to slide the tip into the bag so it poked through the hole in the point of the triangle. Then we stuffed the bag with icing.

"So, you kind of push the icing from the top down while you squeeze," Katie explained. She put some on top of one of the cupcakes in a swirl pattern. It looked really nice.

"Can I try?" I asked.

I tried squeezing some out but I squeezed too hard the first time, and it came out in a big glop.

"Just a little squeeze," Katie told me, and I tried again.

This time I did it better, and a perfect dollop of white icing came out. I covered the top of the cupcake with icing circles, and that looked really nice too.

"We should definitely do this for the show on Saturday," Emma said, and everyone agreed.

"But you mean Sunday," Alexis said.

"Sunday!" Emma cried. "I thought it was Saturday! Sam is in this big basketball tournament on Sunday, and we're all going out of town to cheer him on."

"It's okay, Emma," I said, thinking Dan would probably be there too. Eddie was going to be at the fashion show though. Who would cheer on Dan?

"Ugh, brothers!" Emma said, shrugging at me. "Promise you'll take pictures and text me so I know how it goes?"

"Of course," I said.

"What about the display?" Alexis asked.

"I'll make sure we finish by Saturday," Emma said. "We can work on it this weekend."

Soon we had all the cupcakes finished. Because it was right before dinner, we unwrapped one and cut it into four pieces.

"Mmm, really good," Alexis said.

"I'm thinking a little more nutmeg?" Katie said.

I nodded. "Definitely. They're good, but they need a little more kick. Then they'll be *fabulous*."

Right about then, Eddie came by to bring me home for dinner. I had a small box of our test cupcakes with me for dessert later.

"Did you have a nice time?" Eddie asked when I got in the car.

"It was seriously fantastic," I told him. "The cupcakes came out great, and we're going to make this fabulous display that Mom will love, and we tried a new icing technique."

"That's great," Eddie said. "I bet you girls are going to have a terrific time at the fashion show."

Eddie's remark reminded me—the PGC wanted to go too. I still hadn't figured out what to do about that, but I knew I couldn't put things off much longer. I would have to decide soon and hope nobody got hurt.

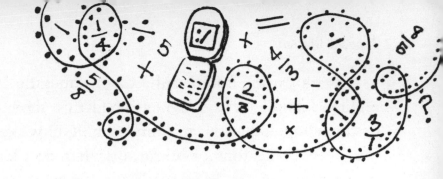

CHAPTER 15

It's Complicated

$\mathcal{F}$riday I took the train to see my dad as usual. We went to Tokyo 16 and then watched a movie when we got home.

The next morning Dad made us omelets and toast. We ate sitting on high stools at the counter that separates the kitchen from the living room. Dad's apartment is big for Manhattan, but the place is pretty small compared to a house in the suburbs. Everything in the kitchen and the living room is either black, silver, or made of glass. My dad's bedroom is like that too. The only color in the house is the pink in my Parisian bedroom.

"So, what are we doing today, *mija*?" Dad asked me as we ate. "Are you going to Ava's soccer game?"

"I've got a big social studies project to do," I replied. I know I haven't mentioned this yet, but besides shopping at the mall and baking cupcakes, I've been doing tons of homework. It seems like there is way more homework now than at my old school. "I don't know if I'll get to see Ava this weekend."

"Why don't we invite her to dinner tonight?" Dad suggested. "I know she loves my chicken."

"What about Alina?" I asked. "Do we have plans with her again?"

"I don't know if I'll be seeing Alina anymore," Dad said. "She and I didn't have as much in common as I thought."

"Hmm. That's too bad," I said. What I really wanted to say was *Hooray! No new stepmom for me! And our walls will be safe too!* But I didn't want to hurt Dad's feelings.

I picked up my dish and put it in the dishwasher. "I'll text Ava about dinner. Then I've got to start on my project. I've got to make this color-coded map showing the most populated countries in the world. It has to have a map key and everything."

"Well, that's right up my alley," Dad said. He's an architect who helps design office buildings, mostly. Dad had a big roll of paper I could use for the map,

114

and he even let me use his special set of colored pencils that I always drool over.

It took me all afternoon to finish the map, but when it was done, it looked great. Mr. Insley, my social studies teacher, would have to give me an A, I just knew it.

Things got even better when Ava came over. Dad made his chicken in tomato sauce, like he promised he would, and we talked and laughed all through dinner.

After we ate, Ava and I went to my bedroom to listen to music. We both flopped down on the floor, and Ava grabbed my sketchbook and started looking through it.

"These are really nice, Mia," Ava said, turning the pages. "I really like the plaid mixed with the flower pattern."

"Thanks!" Ava's always been my biggest fan.

My cell phone beeped, and I flipped it open. There was a text from Sydney.

Want to hang out at my house Monday?

"Who's that?" Ava asked.

"It's Sydney," I replied. "She wants me to hang out at her house on Monday."

"Sydney? I don't remember you talking about her. Is she in the Cupcake Club?"

"No." I propped up a fluffy pink floor pillow against the side of the bed and leaned back. "It's complicated. Sydney formed this club called the Popular Girls Club."

Ava rolled her eyes. "Seriously?"

"I know, but the girls in that club are basically pretty nice," I explained. "And they love to go to the mall with me and talk about fashion. None of my friends in the Cupcake Club are into that."

"So why is it complicated?" Ava asked. "Can't you just be friends with everybody?"

"It's not so easy," I told her. "You see, Katie used to be best friends with Callie, and then Callie dumped Katie to hang out with the PGC. And Alexis kind of hates Sydney, because Sydney's really mean to her, and Emma . . . I think she doesn't like them because she sticks up for Alexis."

"Yeah, things get complicated in middle school." Ava closed the book and sat up. "Like our friends on the soccer team. I love them, but I'm also friends with girls from my dance class. It's not like we all hang out together."

"But it's different," I said. "It's not like the girls

on the soccer team and the girls in your dance class are enemies."

"Maybe not, but I always feel like I'm splitting my time. So are you going to hang out with Sydney?" Ava asked.

I quickly looked at the schedule I keep on my phone. "It doesn't matter if I want to or not, 'cause there's a big math test on Tuesday."

I texted Sydney back.

Math test on Tuesday. Have to study.

I wasn't expecting her reply.

We can study together.

Are u sure? I asked. It's a big test.

Sydney texted back.

Do u want to come or not?

Ava was looking over my shoulder. "Just go. What's the big deal?"

I sighed.

OK. See u Monday.

"It was so much easier when I lived here," I said, flopping backward.

"Well, if you think I've got it easy here, you're wrong," Ava told me. "I have to go halfway across town to get to school. It takes forever. I hardly know anybody. You have, like, a hundred friends already. You're lucky."

I thought about it. Ava might be right. I think I'd rather have too many friends than none at all, even though it can get seriously confusing.

But that didn't make it easier on Monday, when I knew I would see Katie on my way out of school. Katie was waiting for Joanne on the school steps, like she usually was. (I wanted to tell her during lunch, but I just couldn't do it, somehow.)

"Hey!" Katie said. "Joanne's running late today. I wish my mom would just let me take the bus with you."

"Um, I'm not taking the bus today," I said. "I'm going to Sydney's house to study."

Katie looked hurt, but as usual, she tried to act like she wasn't. Right then, Joanne's red car pulled up down the street.

"Okay, cool," she said. "I'll see you tomorrow."

I felt kind of bad. Then I heard Sydney calling me.

"Mia!"

Sydney was on the corner with Bella and Callie. I ran over to meet them.

"Hey," I said. "Where's Maggie?"

"She goes to ballet class on Mondays," Sydney replied. "Her mom thinks it will make her more graceful."

Bella giggled. "I went to her last recital. Poor Maggie. She's hopeless!"

Now that's the diffcrence between the PGC and the Cupcake Club right there. In the Cupcake Club, nobody talks behind anybody else's back.

"I always wanted to take dance lessons," Callie said. "But I was afraid I wouldn't be good at it."

"I like to dance for fun," I said. "Like when we have parties at my aunt's house. We crank up the music and everybody dances—in the kitchen, on the porch, wherever."

"Did you ever go dancing in the dance clubs in New York?" Bella asked.

"No," I said. "You have to be older to do that."

Bella looked disappointed.

"So, are you guys studying with us?" I asked Bella and Callie.

"Mom's taking me to the eye doctor for a follow-up," Callie said. "And then I'm studying tonight."

"And I have . . . other plans," Bella said a little nervously. Sydney was glaring at her. I got the feeling that maybe Sydney had ordered Bella not to hang out with us.

Callie's house was first on the walk home, and then Bella lived a few blocks away. That left me and Sydney. We talked about the new movie starring Ann Harrison that was coming out this weekend. We both think she's gorgeous and seriously talented.

Finally we came to a block that had a lot of old houses like the one Emma lives in. But one house on the block looked brand-new. It was twice as tall as the other houses and it was made of these pinkish-brown smooth stones. There was a big window over the front door and you could see a huge chandelier glimmering through it.

You've probably guessed by now that it was Sydney's house. She took a key from the key chain hanging from her backpack, unlocked the front door, and opened it up.

"Magda! We'd like two sparkling lemonades, please!" Sydney called out.

We walked through the big front hallway (I think it's called a foyer, right?) into a dining room with a gleaming wood table. Another smaller chandelier hung in that room. There was a big cabinet with glass windows with fancy plates and glasses inside. The whole place was sparkling clean.

Sydney dumped her backpack on top of the table and sat down. I sat down across the table from her just as a slim woman with pale blond, pulled-back hair hurried in, carrying two glasses of lemonade. Without a word, she placed them on the table in front of us.

"Thanks!" I said, but Magda quickly left without responding.

"She's not much of a talker," Sydney informed me. "The last housekeeper we had just talked and talked and talked. Mom couldn't take it anymore, so we had to get a new one."

I opened my backpack and took out my math book. "I seriously hate dividing fractions," I said. "It's never made any sense to me. Why do you have to turn the numbers upside down? What's the point?"

Sydney sipped her lemonade. "Yeah, I know. So, tell me about your mom's fashion show. Did she choose the designers yet?"

"I think so," I said. "We're supposed to go over that tonight. I was at my dad's all weekend so we haven't had a chance to talk yet."

"Be right back," Sydney said. She returned a minute later carrying a laptop.

Okay, I thought. *We're going to start studying.*

She typed on the keyboard and turned the screen toward me to show me an image of a model in a long red coat.

"This is perfect for winter, isn't it?" she said.

"It's nice," I agreed. "But we should really study for math now, shouldn't we?"

"One more minute," Sydney said. "We have to check out *Fashionista's* website first. They had a whole spread about Ann Harrison and all her different styles. You have got to see it!"

I was fed up with Sydney's bossiness. I really wanted to study for my math test so I could talk with Mom about the fashion show later. So I did something I wouldn't normally do.

I slipped my math book back into my backpack and stood up. "Listen, Sydney, thanks for inviting me over and everything, but I seriously need to study."

"But it only takes, like, five minutes to go over the review sheet," Sydney said.

"Maybe you only need five minutes, but I need more time," I said. "I'm really, really sorry."

"Okay, whatever." Sydney sounded annoyed.

Great. Now I had hurt two friends in the same day.

As I walked home, I realized I was in the neighborhood where Alexis and Emma lived. I checked the time on my cell phone and saw it wasn't even three thirty yet. So I walked over to Alexis's house and knocked on the door.

Alexis looked surprised to see me. "Hey, Mia. What are you doing here?"

"Well, I was in the neighborhood, and I was wondering if maybe we could study for the math test together," I said.

"Sure. I was just starting," Alexis told me. She motioned for me to come inside.

"Mom! Mia's here! We're studying for math!" Alexis called out. She led me into her kitchen, which was sparkling clean and very, very white. She had her math book and a pad of graph paper spread out on the kitchen table.

Mrs. Becker walked in. She has short hair and glasses and likes to wear mid-length skirts with comfortable-looking shoes. I'd love to give her a makeover some day. She's naturally pretty, but with a makeover she could be a totally hot mom!

"Nice to see you, Mia," she said. "There are bananas and apples on the counter if you're hungry."

"Thanks, Mrs. Becker," I said.

Alexis and I got right down to business. By four thirty, I was almost an expert in dividing fractions. I even knew what a "reciprocal" was. Amazing.

"You should become a teacher," I told Alexis. "I actually feel like I understand this stuff."

Alexis blushed. "Yeah, I think about that sometimes. Want a banana?"

I nodded, and she went to the counter and grabbed a banana for each of us.

"Thanks so much for studying with me," I said as I peeled my banana. "Mom's going crazy getting ready for this fashion show, and we're supposed to meet to talk about it today."

"What's making her crazy?" Alexis asked.

"There's just so much to be done," I said. "Getting the food, making the seating chart, hiring the models, deciding which model will wear what look . . ."

Alexis started sketching on a piece of graph paper. "Why don't you make a flowchart? That's what I always do when I have a lot to do."

I looked over her shoulder. "That is pretty awesome. Can I show my mom?"

"Sure," Alexis replied. "Or how about this? I can do a blank one on the computer and send it to you."

"Oh my gosh, that would be fabulous!" I said. "Alexis, you are the best!"

Alexis grinned. "Let me know if you need any help at the fashion show, okay? I don't know anything about fashion, but I'm good at organizing things. I could always stay after we set up the cupcakes."

"Thanks. I'll ask my mom," I said.

As I walked home, I thought about how different Alexis was from Sydney. If I were having a friend contest, Alexis definitely would have won the prize today.

Maybe things weren't really as complicated as I thought.

CHAPTER 16

A Big Deal

$\mathcal{M}$om was thrilled with the flowcharts Alexis e-mailed me.

"Alexis did these?" she asked in disbelief. "I should hire this girl as my assistant."

"Hey, I thought *I* was your assistant," I said.

"You're my number one *fashion* assistant," Mom promised. "But I do need someone to help keep me organized."

"Alexis said she would help out if you wanted," I told her.

"Maybe," Mom said. "But fashion first! Let me show you the outfits and accessories I've got so far."

Mom had gotten a lot done over the weekend. In her office were two racks filled with clothes and a few large plastic bins filled with shoes, bags, and jewelry. Mom and I spent two hours matching dresses and jackets, shirts and skirts, pants and tops, and picking out accessories for each look. We still hadn't finished when I started yawning.

"Sorry, sweetie, I didn't realize how late it was getting," Mom said. "I'll finish up here. You need to rest for that big math test tomorrow."

I don't know what I was more nervous about— my math test or facing Sydney after walking out on her. But I shouldn't have worried. When I saw Sydney in homeroom, she flashed me that toothpaste-commercial smile of hers.

"Hey, study nerd," she said. "Were you up all night getting ready for the test?"

"No," I admitted. "But I think I'm ready for it."

"Of course you are," Sydney said. "So, you owe me after yesterday. Sit with us at lunch, okay?"

I could picture the hurt look on Katie's face if I accepted, but it was hard for me to refuse after everything that happened.

"Cool, thanks."

I ended up acing the math test, thanks in part to Alexis. She was really a good teacher. Either that or math was starting to make sense.

I got to lunch early so I could talk to Katie. I caught her by the front door.

127

"Hey, Katie," I said. "I need to tell you something."

"Let me guess," Katie said. "You're sitting with the PGC today."

"You're right," I said. "I kind of have to. I was sort of rude to Sydney yesterday and left her house like five minutes after I got there. But I'm not changing tables permanently or anything."

Katie didn't look directly at me, and I knew she was upset. She doesn't like to say how she's really feeling, though.

"You're the best friend I've made since I moved here," I told her.

Katie smiled a little bit. "Okay. Have fun talking about boring clothes." She rolled her eyes in a funny way, and I knew she was teasing.

"Thanks," I said. "I'll talk to you later."

The rest of the PGC girls were sitting down when I got to the table. Maggie rushed over to me.

"Oh, Mia, Mia, Mia!" she said. "Say it isn't true!"

"Say what isn't true?" I asked.

"My mom told me that tickets to your mom's fashion show are all sold out," she said. "But that can't be true, can it?"

"Maybe—I mean, I'm not sure," I said. "She didn't say anything."

"But we can still go, right?" Sydney asked.

"I still have to find out," I said. I had put off asking my Mom last night, because I still didn't know what to do.

Callie changed the subject. "So, how was the math test?"

Thankfully nobody mentioned the fashion show again for the rest of lunch, so that was good.

With the math test off of my mind, I was able to concentrate on cupcakes. I had no idea how to decorate the tops of the cupcakes for the fashion show. After school I went up to my room and started looking online for ideas.

Somehow I came across this site for a baking supply store. They had tons and tons of stuff, and two things caught my eye. They had these little pieces of candied ginger that would look just like jewels on top of the chocolate cupcakes. They also had red cinnamon-flavored sugar that looked like glitter. How cool would that be on top of the white frosting on the applesauce cupcakes? And perfect for Mom's spicy theme too.

But it was already Tuesday, and there was no way they would get here in time if I ordered them— at least, that's what I thought. When I checked the contact page, I saw that the store was in

Springfield—right over in the next town!

I ran downstairs as fast as I could. Dan was at the kitchen table doing homework, and Mom was chopping vegetables for dinner.

"Mom, I found this awesome baking supply shop in Springfield," I said. "It's got the perfect decorations for the cupcakes for your show. Can you take me there tonight? They're open till eight."

"Oh sweetie, I've got to go to the banquet hall tonight to work out the floor plan," Mom said. "I'm so sorry. I know Eddie would take you, but he's working late tonight."

Dan looked up from his book. "I'll take you," he said.

I was surprised. "Really? You don't mind?"

Dan shook his head. "We can go after dinner."

Mom gave him a huge smile. "Dan, that's so sweet of you. Thanks!"

So right after dinner I was driving to Cake Sensations in Dan's red sports car that used to belong to his uncle. He'd been driving it around ever since he got his license last month. I was sure that's why he agreed to drive me.

But as we rode along, I figured out he had another reason.

"So, I'm sorry I ruined your shirt," he said. "I

didn't mean to. I'm just used to dumping everything in the laundry basket into the machine at once. It's just everything's you know . . . different now."

He didn't sound mad when he said that last sentence, or sad, either. But something about how he said it made me think again that it must be weird for him, too. I guess we were all adjusting to the changes.

"It's okay," I said. "It's just a shirt."

It didn't take long to get to Springfield.

"The directions say to take a left onto Main Street," I told Dan.

Dan slowed down and put on his blinker. "Hey, I know this place," he said. "It's right next to the doctor where I get my shots."

"Shots? What shots?" I asked.

"You know, for the dogs," Dan said. "I'm allergic to them, so I have to get shots."

Why hadn't I heard this before? "Seriously? I didn't know that. You mean you have to get shots because of Tiki and Milkshake?"

Dan shrugged. "It's okay. They don't hurt. Besides, I like those dogs."

Dan parked the car in front of Cake Sensations, and when we got out, I walked over to him and gave him a hug.

"Uh, thanks," Dan said. "But it's just a short ride. It's no big deal."

But I wasn't hugging him just because of the ride. "It *is* a big deal," I said. "Thanks."

CHAPTER 17

Mixing It Up

I bought a jar of the glittery cinnamon sugar and a container of small pieces of candied ginger at the Cake Sensations store. Dan used the calculator on his cell phone to divide the cost between eight dozen cupcakes, and I came in at nineteen cents per cupcake. Alexis would be so proud of me!

When we got home, Dan went into his room and blasted his music, but I didn't mind it as much as I usually do. I put on my headphones and did a little sketching before bedtime. I was about to change into my pajamas when Mom opened the door.

"Well, that went smoothly, thank goodness," she said. "Those charts Alexis made really helped. Please thank her for me."

"You can thank her tomorrow," I said. "Everyone's coming over after school to do a test batch of the chocolate spice cupcakes, remember?"

"Oh, right!" Mom said. "Hey, that reminds me. I saved three front-row tickets for you to give to your friends."

Mom looked through her purse and came up with three tickets printed on red paper, which she handed to me. "They're the last three tickets I've got."

"Thanks, Mom," I said. I got up and gave her a hug.

Mom kissed my cheek. "Get a good night's sleep, sweetie."

She left, and I looked at the three tickets in my hand. I knew how badly Sydney wanted to go. But if they belonged to anyone, it was the Cupcake Club.

Katie, Alexis, Emma. I wrote their names down in my sketchbook. Then I remembered that Emma wasn't going to be there.

Katie, Alexis . . . Sydney? Yikes. That would never work.

I tried thinking another way. Katie and Alexis had never once asked me for tickets to the show. They probably didn't even want to go.

Sydney, Maggie, Bella, Callie. That was one girl too many. But which girl would I leave out? I liked Callie, so she could stay. Sydney would be furious if I left her out. That left Maggie or Bella, and I didn't want to hurt either of their feelings. They'd always been nice to me.

And then, how would Katie and Alexis feel if I didn't even offer them the tickets? Maybe they didn't ask because they just assumed they were going. . . .

Frustrated, I closed the sketchbook. I didn't want to think about it anymore. Maybe the decision would come to me in a dream. . . .

It didn't. I still hadn't made any decisions by the time the Cupcake Club came over the next day after school. Katie brought the ingredients with her, and I was really excited to show everyone what I had found at Cake Sensations.

"See this glittery sugar? It's cinnamon flavored," I said. "I think it will look so pretty on the apple-sauce cupcakes, and it matches the red display."

"It's perfect!" Emma agreed.

"And these are little pieces of candied ginger." I picked up one of the little orange jewels. "I thought they'd be good for the chocolate spice cupcakes, since there's ginger inside."

"That's going to look really cool," Alexis said. "Hey, can I crack the eggs this time?"

"The eggs are all yours," Katie said, handing her the carton.

But before we started baking, Mom came into the kitchen holding some papers in her hand.

"Hi, girls," she said. "I thought I'd show you where the cupcake table's going to be set up on Sunday."

She spread out the papers on the table. They showed a floorplan of the banquet hall.

"See, there's the runway," she said. "And these are the seats. And the refreshments will be over here."

"Where does everyone check in?" Alexis asked.

"What do you mean?" Mom asked.

"You know, like where they turn in their tickets and get their seat assignment," she replied.

Mom turned pale. "Oh, no! I didn't think of that."

Alexis pointed to the layout. "I think right here's the perfect spot for it. I'm sure the banquet hall can set up one more table for you."

Mom hugged Alexis. "You are a genius! Mia said you'd be willing to help out during the show. Would you work the check-in table for me?"

Alexis looked thrilled. "I would love to! That would be fun."

"Thank you, thank you, thank you!" Mom said. She quickly picked up the papers. "I need to go call the banquet hall right now."

"I wish I was going," Emma said after Mom left.

"I'll text you photos, I promise," I told her.

"Stupid game," Emma muttered. That reminded me about Dan. But just then Katie leaned over the counter.

"I was meaning to ask you," Katie said. "Can I stay and watch the show after we set up the cupcakes?"

"Um, I just need to find out if Mom is going to give me tickets," I lied.

Katie shrugged. "Cool. It sounds like fun, but as long as the cupcakes are perfect, I'll be happy."

My mind was racing. Alexis didn't need a ticket. I really needed to give Katie one. That left two. *Katie, Callie, Sydney?* Way awkward.

Katie measured the flour and dumped it into the bowl.

"Okay, now we need a teaspoon of powdered ginger and two tablespoons of cocoa powder," she said. "And then we need to mix them up."

Emma added the spices, and Katie started

stirring the ingredients with a whisk. She did a groovy dance. "Oh yeah. Mix it up, mix it up," she sang.

Then it hit me. *Mix it up.* When you mix the wrong ingredients together, the result can be a disaster. But when you mix the right ingredients together, everything comes out delicious.

Suddenly everything was clear.

I knew exactly who to give the three tickets to.

CHAPTER 18

A Little Sweetness in the End

"Ninety-five, ninety-six," Alexis counted, placing the last cupcake on top of the display.

Katie, Alexis, and I took a step back and admired our work. It had taken all of us (plus Emma) all day and part of the night on Saturday to make all ninety-six cupcakes. They looked beautiful. And the displays Emma and her dad made were really cool, just like I imagined them. The two red towers were simple, but they were the perfect accent for the colorful tablecloths Mom had chosen for the refreshment tables.

"Let me get a picture for Emma," I said, taking a quick shot with my phone and sending it to her.

The displays are perfect! U r the best!

Thanks! Emma texted back. Miss u guys! I'll text you the pictures on this end too!

Katie started gathering up the empty cupcake carriers.

"I'll help you," Alexis offered.

"Cool." Katie nodded to me. "See you later!"

It was just two hours before the fashion show, and things were getting pretty crazy in the banquet hall. The DJ was setting up his equipment in the back corner, and Mom was on the runway talking to a guy about the lights. She climbed down when she noticed that we had finished the display.

"Wow, Mia, that's fabulous," Mom said. "These look delicious."

"Thanks," I said.

"Listen, the models are starting to arrive. Can you start helping them get dressed? I'll be back there in a minute." She handed me a clipboard with Alexis's charts on it.

"Sure, Mom," I said. I've been backstage with Mom at fashion shows since I can remember, but this was the first time she was actually letting me help. I didn't want to let her down.

I headed to the curtain behind the runway. It separated the banquet hall into two spaces—the show area and the backstage area. The models would be getting changed in the room behind the curtain.

Thankfully, the charts made things pretty easy. As soon as I walked backstage, a model with long, glossy black hair walked up to me.

"Is Sara Vélaz here?" she asked.

"I'm her daughter, Mia," I said in my most professional voice. "Can you please give me your name?"

"It's Lori," the model told me.

I found her name on the chart and started walking to the racks of clothes. Each model had a picture of the outfit she'd be wearing under her name on a wall. And each model had a rack with all the outfits hung on them. I found "Lori" on the card taped over one rack. "Here are the clothes you'll be wearing," I told her. "The red dress is your first outfit. Please head to the makeup room first."

I pointed toward the large ladies' room, where Mom had the makeup artists set up.

"Thanks, Mia," Lori said. "You know, you're a lot like your mom."

The next two hours went by really fast. The models started coming in, and Mom and I helped each one get ready. There were all kinds of problems: One shirt was too big, one skirt was too short,

141

one model had on the wrong earrings—stuff like that.

In the middle of it all Ray, the DJ, came backstage.

"Sara, one of the outlets just lost power," he said.

Mom looked at her watch. "Oh, great. The show starts in twenty minutes." She turned to me. "Mia, can you go to the main office and ask for Ernie? He should be able to help with this."

"Sure, Mom," I told her. I ducked out a nearby door that led into a hallway that bypassed the main room because I knew it would be faster and less crowded. I could see the check-in table up ahead. Alexis had her back to me and was talking with three guests.

Then I heard Sydney's loud voice. "But I'm *sure* Mia put us on the list."

My heart pounding, I ducked behind a big pillar and listened to what was going on.

"Sydney, I'm sorry, but your name isn't on this list," Alexis said. "Or Maggie or Bella, either."

"That's impossible. Mia told us all about the show," Sydney said. She sounded really mad. "And where is Callie, anyway?"

"There's nothing I can do for you. The show is sold out," Alexis explained patiently.

"Of course you can do something. You can go find Mia for me," Sydney insisted.

"Give me a second," Alexis replied.

My cell phone buzzed in my pocket. I quickly shut it off. Like it or not, I would have to face the music. I stepped out from behind the pillar and walked up to the check-in table.

Sydney was done up to the max, wearing a black dress with a bubble skirt and black heels. She had her hair swept up on her head and had tons of per-fume on.

"There she is!" Sydney said, pointing at me.

"Mia? I just tried to reach your phone," Alexis said, looking confused. "Anyway, Sydney and Maggie and Bella keep saying you put them on the list." Alexis looked at me.

"I know," I said. I felt awful. "Listen, I'm really sorry about this, but I just didn't have enough tickets for everyone who wanted to come," I said weakly.

Sydney just stared at me.

"But you promised we could come!" Maggie wailed.

"I didn't promise anything," I replied. "But I should have told you about the tickets earlier. I'm so sorry. I really am."

Then I had an idea. "Hey, why don't you come backstage and help out? I can ask my mom if it's all right. It's a really cool way to see the show."

Sydney looked horrified. "We came to watch the show, not *work* it," she said, with a disgusted look in Alexis's direction. "Mia, I don't know how you could do this to a friend. We were seriously considering you for a membership in the PGC, but we're going to have to reevaluate your membership status now."

"Well, my friends don't *evaluate* one another," I shot back.

Sydney stormed off without another word, with Maggie and Bella following behind.

I turned to Alexis, embarrassed. "Don't worry about it, everyone makes mistakes . . . even me!" Alexis said. She was trying really hard not to laugh. "Hey, shouldn't you be backstage helping your mom?"

I slapped my hand on my forehead. "Oh, no! I've got to find Ernie!"

Luckily, Ernie was in his office, and he quickly followed me backstage. I helped Mom with the rest of the models, and a few minutes later Ernie came back.

"You're all set, Ms. Vélaz," he told Mom.

Mom turned to me. "Deep breath," she said, and we both took a deep breath at once. "Okay. I'm on."

Mom stepped out onto the stage and the noisy crowd quieted down. I walked to the end of the curtain and quietly slipped through so I could watch.

"Thank you so much for coming, everyone!" she said. "I'm Sara Vélaz, and today you're going to see some of the latest fashions from top designers. We've carefully crafted the looks today to show you how you can add some key pieces to spice up your wardrobe."

Everyone clapped.

"And after the show, please stay for a little sweetness, courtesy of the Cupcake Club," Mom said, pointing to the refreshments table.

I realized then that my mom could have hired anyone to cater her first big event, but she chose us. I guess it was her way of including my latest hobby and new friends. Mom was really trying to help everything fit in together.

I looked out to the side and saw Eddie standing in the back. He looked really proud. He was taking pictures and videos of everything. Which reminded me . . . I turned on my phone. Sure enough, there was a picture from Emma of her brother Jake holding the sign I made: GO, DAN GO! And there was a text from Dan:

Thx sis. Save me a cupcake.

I couldn't help but smile at being called "sis."

I looked out at the front row and gave a little wave to my three friends sitting there: Katie, Callie, and Ava. My best friend from the Cupcake Club, my best friend from the PGC, and my best friend from New York. The perfect mix.

I still haven't totally figured out how to mix *everything* from my old life and my new life together, but that's okay. This is good enough for now, and so far, the results are pretty sweet.

If you're not an expert baker like Mia, that's okay—here is a quick and easy-to-follow recipe that's just as sweet! (Ask an adult for assistance before you start baking since you might need help with the oven or mixer.)

Vanilla Cupcakes with Vanilla Buttercream Frosting

• Makes 12 •

BATTER:
½ cup unsalted butter, at room temperature
⅔ cup granulated sugar
3 large eggs, at room temperature
1 teaspoon pure vanilla extract
1 ½ cups all-purpose flour
1 ½ teaspoons baking powder
¼ teaspoon salt
¼ cup whole milk

FROSTING:
½ cup unsalted butter, at room temperature
4 cups sifted confectioners' sugar
⅓ cup of whole milk
1 teaspoon pure vanilla extract
food coloring (optional)

Center baking rack in oven and preheat to 350°F. Line cupcake tins with cupcake liners.

CUPCAKES: In a medium bowl, beat the butter and sugar with an electric mixer on medium speed until fluffy. Then add the eggs one at a time. Blend in the vanilla extract.

In a separate bowl whisk together the flour, baking powder, and salt. With the mixer on low speed, add the flour mixture to the butter-sugar mixture and alternate with the milk. Mix until there are no lumps in the batter.

Evenly fill the cupcake tins with the batter and bake for about 18 to 20 minutes or until a toothpick inserted into the center of a cupcake comes out clean. Remove from oven and place on a wire rack to cool completely before frosting.

FROSTING: In a medium bowl mix the butter with an electric mixer until it looks fluffy. Add in some of the sugar, alternating with the milk and vanilla until it is all blended. Add food coloring per package's directions and mix well to color the frosting. Then frost the cupcakes.

$\mathcal{W}$ant another sweet cupcake?

Here's a sneak peek

of the third book in the

CUPCAKE 🧁 DIARIES

series:

Emma

on thin

icing

Great News!

*M*y name is Emma Taylor, and my life can be pretty hectic sometimes. I have three brothers, four goldfish, a guinea pig, and two jobs. Yup—two businesses. The first is a dog-walking job I have after school. My other job isn't really a job. It's a club with my best friends—Alexis, Katie, and Mia. Together we're the Cupcake Club. We bake and sell cupcakes for different people and events. It's totally fun, but we don't earn that much money . . . yet.

Between my brothers, chores, and the club, things can get pretty crazy. Most of the time, though, being in the middle of all this craziness can mean getting some pretty great inspirations. Like the one I had about bacon. Bacon cupcakes. Trust me—they're great. They're salty with the bacon and sweet with the sugar, and the combination is really the best. It just *sounds* gross. I had been waiting to bring it up until just the right time, and finally, at our club meeting, I decided to see how it would fly. We were talking about new ideas because we're always trying out new things, depending on the event. I was a little nervous, but I decided to float the idea.

"Okay, ready? How about . . . bacon cupcakes?" I asked.

I spread my arms wide in an arc—like "ta-da"— as I announced my idea. I wasn't sure how the others would react to it, but I thought it was pretty neat. And original. That was for sure. I just hoped they didn't think I was nuts.

"Ewwww!" cried Katie, with a full body shudder.

"Are you kidding me?" Alexis looked so horrified you would have thought I had suggested road-kill cupcakes.

I just shrugged. I knew better. "My brothers loved them. I made them last week. Actually, they're delicious. Kind of salty and sweet. Think about it."

Unlike the other members of the Cupcake Club, Mia was quiet, and she looked like she was actually considering the idea. Finally she said, "I love bacon *and* cupcakes, but I've never thought about them together. Bacon is kinda in right now. There's bacon gum, bacon mayonnaise, bacon ice cream, bacon-shaped Band-Aids. It would be pretty cool to have bacon cupcakes."

Mia was pretty hip. She had long, straight, dark hair and really cool outfits, and she was from Manhattan. I have no idea how she knew what was "in" or what wasn't, but we all pretty much listened when she said something was in. So Katie and Alexis stopped their dramatic groaning and belly clutching and listened.

Seeing that I was making headway with my idea, I forged on. "I was thinking, maybe for the groom's cake. You know how they do that? Have a special cake on the side? It's kind of a Southern thing. The bride has her own cake and the groom has his."

"Like an extra order?" asked Katie.

I nodded and looked a little guiltily at Mia. "Not that I want to make money off your mom or anything."

"Emma, you may have just doubled our revenue!" said Alexis, ever the businesswoman. She raised her glass of Gatorade in a toast. I smiled and raised my glass back at her. Alexis actually did look like a businesswoman right now, with her red hair up in a bun, and she was wearing a sensible button-down shirt and holding a calculator and a pad of paper.

The Cupcake Club was meeting in Mia's cozy TV room to brainstorm about upcoming jobs. One of our next big events was Mia's mom's wedding to Eddie, her supernice fiancé. We were all excited for Mia because Eddie was great and her mom was really happy. But we were also excited for ourselves because Mia's mom had placed an order with the club for cupcakes for the wedding! She had given us the green light to do whatever we thought was appropriate—if bacon cupcakes were appropriate. Best of all, she would pay us for the order.

Alexis was taking notes. "Okay, let me just read this back to you. One idea is a circular cupcake wedding cake built with three sizes of cupcakes to make up the tiers—our medium, large, and jumbo sizes building out the cake, with a few minis on top. The cake would be white; the frosting would be white buttercream. Decorations would be white flowers molded from edible fondant. Cupcake papers would be shiny and white." She looked up at the other Cupcake Club members for confirmation. We all nodded, and she looked back at her notes.

"Another idea is to do all minis laid out in a

large sheet, mostly white cake and white frosting but with select cupcakes frosted in pink raspberry frosting and placed to form the shape of a heart in the middle of the layout." Again we nodded. The mini cupcakes were very popular; they were not much bigger than a quarter, and they could be consumed easily in vast quantities.

Alexis continued. "We will also submit a bid for a groom's cake made of . . . um, bacon cupcakes. These are . . . what kind of cake?"

"Caramel cake," I said. My mouth was watering just thinking of it. "And the frosting is just a standard buttercream with flecks of real bacon in it. It comes out sort of beige."

Alexis shuddered. "Okay. Beige cupcakes. I will do an analysis on head count and budget and come up with a cupcake count so we can submit our bids to your mom by the end of the week. I'll e-mail it to everyone for approval first. Especially the bacon cupcake part. Then we can meet and go over it again."

We nodded in agreement.

"Next on the agenda is—"

"Wait!" interrupted Mia, her eyes shining with excitement. "I have great news."

Still Hungry?
There's always room for another Cupcake!

Katie and the Cupcake Cure
1

Mia in the Mix
2

Emma on Thin Icing
3

Alexis and the Perfect Recipe
4

Katie, Batter Up!
5

Mia's Baker's Dozen
6

Emma All Stirred Up!
7

Alexis Cool as a Cupcake
8

Katie and the Cupcake War
9

Mia's Boiling Point
10

Emma, Smile and Say "Cupcake!"
11

Alexis Gets Frosted
12

Katie's New Recipe
13

Mia a Matter of Taste
14